About the author

Ajay K Pandey grew up in the modest NTPC township of Rihand Nagar with big dreams. He studied Engineering in Electronics at IERT (Allahabad) and MBA at IIMM (Pune) before taking up a job in a corporate firm.

He grew up with a dream of becoming a teacher, but destiny landed him in the IT field. Travelling, trekking and reading novels are his hobbies. Travelling to different places has taught him about different cultures and people, and makes him wonder how despite all the differences, there is a bond that unites them. Trekking always inspires him to deal with challenges like a sport. Reading is perhaps what makes him feel alive.

You are the Best Wife was his debut book based on his life events and lessons. Apart from writing, he wants to follow his role model Mother Teresa and create a charitable trust to support aged people and educate special children.

After his debut book, Ajay has authored bestselling titles *Her Last Wish, You Are the Best Friend, An Unexpected Gift* and *A Girl to Remember.*

: AuthorAjayPandey   : @AjayPandey_08
: @author_ajaykpandey   : ajaypandey0807@gmail.com

By the same author

You Are the Best Wife

Her Last Wish

A Girl to Remember

Praise for the author and his works

"Can an IT professional write bestselling books? Ajay Pandey, the author of two bestsellers would have an answer to this."

— The Hindu

"Bhavna's last words become strength for Ajay, who lives to fulfil his promise of love."

— Business Standard

"... channelise his agony into writing. The result? Two bestselling novels, You Are the Best Wife and Her Last Wish, based on a true love story.

— The Asian Age

"... a semi-autobiographical book on vanquishing loneliness."

— Mid-Day

"... anyone who is going through a rough phase in terms of a personal relationship must read this."

— Deccan Chronicle

"... Pandey beat the likes of JK Rowling and Devdutt Pattanaik to go to the top of the bestselling list in India."

— Mid-Day

"... Ajay K Pandey hit the big league of pulpy romance."

— Quartz India

"... a bestselling book is made."

— Scroll.in

"The real love story will pull you in a pool of emotions."

— *Jagran*

"There are some books that are not just stories but reflection of realities of life. You are the Best Wife is one such book.

— *WritersMelon*

"The Indian author has given reasons to believe that India has not only given good tech-heads, but are delivering literary moths too."

— *The Truth India*

"...sold over a lakh copies... connected with the masses in a way no previous author has ever done."

— *BookGeeks.in*

"The loving heart of a beautiful soul Bhavna, encouraged Ajay to fight back and start looking at life in a positive way."

— *India Café 24*

"It is one of the purest, heart-warming love stories I ever read..."

— *Salisonline.in*

Everything
I Never
Told You

Ajay K Pandey

Srishti
PUBLISHERS & DISTRIBUTORS

Srishti Publishers & Distributors
A unit of AJR Publishing LLP
212A, Peacock Lane
Shahpur Jat, New Delhi – 110 049
editorial@srishtipublishers.com

First published by
Srishti Publishers & Distributors in 2020

Copyright © Ajay K Pandey, 2020

10 9

Cover concept: Saurabh Garge. Cover picture: Pixabay

Printed and bound in India

Dedicated to Mr Roshan Dixit.
Thanks for allowing me to make
modifications in your story.

We can live without a religion, but we cannot survive without human emotions.

–Soha

Acknowledgement

Hi friends,

The idea of writing this book sprouted when I met Roshan and Soha. I was so taken in with how these two have made their love story a success. I have been wanting to write about their story and struggle ever since. However, I have changed a big chunk of their real life experiences into fiction for this book.

My deepest respect to my entire family that stood by me and decided to take each step with me.

Heartfelt gratitude to the exceptional team at Srishti Publishers for the superb guidance, with a special mention of Jayanta Bose, Arup Bose and Stuti.

Love and thanks to Merril Anil for her contribution to the book.

Many thanks to my friends from the film world – Adit Singh and Prashant Bhagia.

Thank you, Satish and Gautam sir for showing your faith in me.

A big thank you to my readers for accepting my crazy stories.

I am quite active on Instagram and Twitter. Please do connect. I make it a point to reply to each and every message and comment that I get. Believe it or not, it is you who have made me what I am today.

I take this opportunity to thank all the wonderful hearts who stood in my support in their own individual way. Your reviews and feedback are the *silent but efficient way to promote an author. Thank you for making me an author, though I would always politely ask you to treat me as your author friend.*

Never surrender!
Ajay

1

Roshan

‘**A**re you sure you want to do this?’ Soha asked for the sixth time. She knew very well how difficult it had been for me back then. And now, even after all those years, it was still almost impossible.

We had been discussing the same thing for the last few hours. Was it morally wrong? I was not sure. Life seemed to have come full circle. I had been in this situation in the past too. Back then, it was Soha's father. Now, I had to face my own son.

‘Am I doing something wrong?’ I asked Soha, noticing the obvious worry on her face.

‘It is not about right or wrong, Roshan. It's just that sometimes, it is impossible to make people understand... to make them see things from your perspective.’

‘But so much has changed since then, Soha.’

‘Oh yes, it has. Back then, you were twenty-five. Now, you are almost forty-five years old.’

‘I am forty-six, and a couple of years older to you.’ I smiled.

'Oh! We are old.' She smiled back.

A lot was said in that one statement, without any words. I looked into Soha's eyes and saw all the years between us, the years we had lived without each other.

'Will you be able to face the society?' she asked.

'I will face everyone.'

I knew she was checking my confidence. She went into the kitchen, cleaned our now-empty coffee mugs and placed the coffee and sugar jars back to their shelves. She moved around the house like she had always belonged here. In the midst of all this, she kept looking at the clock. Anuj would be home from school any time now, and it was obvious that she was in a hurry to leave. She did not want to face Anuj.

Anuj, my seventeen-year-old son is the only treasure in my life. I lost my wife Manisha four years back, when Anuj was just about fourteen. He was a darling to his mother, and his overly-emotional teenage mind and heart took a long time to come to terms with the loss. Even in Manisha's last days, Anuj refused to leave her side. It badly affected his studies and I had to send him to Alisha's house often. Alisha was Anuj's maasi, Manisha's younger sister. She was the only mother figure in Anuj's life now.

'Okay, I have to reach the clinic. I won't be able to come tomorrow, because I have a surgery scheduled,' Soha said, collecting her belongings and searching for her shoes. She was a gynaecologist, running a clinic in Rohini. Strangely, she had been certain about her life goals, even as a child. She had always dreamt of becoming a doctor.

There was no fatigue in her personality, even though she had been managing that clinic single-handedly for ten years now. Her elder brother was settled in Germany, leaving her to be the sole owner of everything that earlier belonged to her father, Dr Khan. I often wondered how she would have managed all that alone. But I knew her well. One of her traits that stood out and helped her beat the world was – she had mastered the art of saying no to others. She knew that saying no to others often meant saying yes to herself.

She hailed from an affluent Muslim family and her father always stood by her decisions, like a rock solid support. Late Dr Khan used to be a leading surgeon at Noor Clinic in Rohini. He had built the clinic from scratch and Soha was practicing in the same clinic. After her father passed away, she took over the clinic and expanded it to make it better equipped and all-encompassing. Today, Noor Clinic, with its two-storied building, was much more than a small clinic that it once used to be.

We grew up together, studied together, laughed together and even struggled together. In fact, a lot happened in my life after we parted ways. Everything changed in an unrecognizable way. Although I was not the same person anymore, it seemed life hadn't been able to change her much. She was just the same, how she used to be so many years back.

She broke my chain of thoughts with, 'I am leaving, Roshan.' I nodded in response.

'You will have to talk to Anuj today.'

'Yes.' How could I forget!

'I have a suggestion for you,' she said calmly, looking into my eyes without blinking.

'I don't think I am in the mood to hear any today.'

'I know, but just one last thing.' She had always been like this – unstoppable. She was an ocean of advice.

'Alright, say it, please. You won't be able to rest in peace otherwise,' I gave in.

'You should talk to your son more often...' Before she could finish her sentence, there was a knock at the door.

'Shit!' Soha panicked.

'Relax, there is nothing to worry.' Anuj knew Soha, but he had never asked me anything about her.

'I am not ready to face him,' Soha said softly. I did not react and opened the door, although I was a little nervous myself.

Anuj stood at the door. His eyes met mine and then landed on Soha. His face turned stiff for a moment, but he walked in and took a deep breath.

'Namaste auntie!' He greeted her with a poker face.

'Hi beta, how are you doing? Hope you are taking those medicines I gave you for fitness. Oh, and congratulations for your exam results. Roshan told me you've done really well,' Soha said along with the usual pleasantries.

His formal greetings had unceremonious hesitations. He nodded and moved directly to the washroom.

'I will leave now, Roshan,' Soha broke the eerie silence in the room.

I nodded, unable to say anything else amidst the awkwardness that was choking both of us.

I knew it was an unexpected situation. I had wanted Soha to meet Anuj, but unfortunately, not this way. I went into the kitchen to make some coffee for Anuj.

Anuj was still in the washroom. I realised he was taking longer than usual and it worried me a little. I went near the washroom door, to make sure he was fine. It seemed like he was struggling to breathe, had ragged and uneven breathing. Was he sobbing? After a few seconds, there was dead silence. I wanted to break open the door. I raised my hand to knock at the door, but it opened just then. His red eyes and face soaked in disappointment spoke volumes.

'Sorry, something had fallen into my eyes. You can use the washroom now,' he told me and moved to the couch. He dug out his phone and stared into the screen. I stood fixed outside the washroom, while he pretended to be occupied on his mobile.

I sat next to him and tried to look at his phone screen. He was re-tweeting some tweet about how Hindus are in danger. I placed my hand on his shoulder, but he did not react to it. It seemed Twitter was more important to him than I was.

Today was a big day for him. He had topped in the class XII results that were recently declared. I was hoping he would come home beaming. But more than anything, he looked glum.

'How are you, Anuj? How was your last day at school?'

'It was good. They gave me the "Best Student" award and invited me to the annual day celebrations.'

'That is good.' I tried to cheer him up.

Then why were you crying in the washroom? I wanted to ask with all my heart, but couldn't summon the courage.

'Papa, I am getting late for the gym,' he said, getting up.

'Wait, Anuj! I want to talk to you.'

'About what, Papa?' He still held his phone, deliberately avoiding eye contact.

I guess we both understood what the topic of discussion was going to be. He gave me an expression which said I was wasting his precious time.

'Anuj, I am sure you are mature enough to understand this... now that you are going to be eighteen soon.'

'What happened, Papa?' He stopped staring at his phone and looked directly at me.

Anyone could make out that he had been crying with one look at his red eyes. I had no idea why we did not talk as much as we could have. He was so close to his mom, and when he got to know she had cancer, he spent a lot of his time with Alisha. I was so busy with managing and balancing the finances and work, that I lost out on a lot with him.

'Beta, why were you crying in the washroom?'

'Is that really what you wanted to talk about?'

'No.'

I took in a long breath and memories of years ago came flooding. Of the time when I was equally nervous, when I had to speak to Soha's father.

'Son, I wanted to discuss something really important.' He made a face, but I wanted to make sure I spoke to him clearly, in detail. 'When your mom left us, she took a lot with her. I loved her. I still love her.'

'Papa, I have a request. If possible, do not involve mom in this,' he interrupted me.

I understood that I had to come straight to the point before things went horribly wrong between us.

'I want to get married.'

His red eyes and stiff face gave me a heart-piercing look. 'Are you asking for my consent or informing me?'

He had never spoken to me like that. I am an advocate by profession, and have had my fair share of heated arguments and angry faces, but this was different.

'I want your support in my decision, Anuj.'

He took out his phone and checked notifications. A few seconds later, he stood up and started walking away.

'Don't you want to know who the person is?' I called out.

'I know that at this age, my father wants to marry a Muslim woman.'

2
Anuj

Hi, I am Anuj. You must be thinking what an awful person I am. That's why I am here... to tell you my version of the story.

My XII standard exam results were just announced and I had topped my class. I wanted to celebrate, but couldn't, because my heart was not in it. I lost my mother four years ago, but it was a wound that still bled.

I had already secured admission in Birla Institute of Technology for Engineering. The session was to begin in August, which meant I still had two long months in hand. I thought it would be the best time – since I had nothing to study for now, and could spend my time as I wanted – but everything changed that one evening.

My school principal had invited me to school to celebrate my success. He presented me to the entire school as an example to be followed. It was a dream moment. Hundreds of students and friends shook hands with me and hugged me. The teachers were so proud, and I felt on top of the world.

I came home from school, joyous and eager to share my success with my father, and I found him with Soha auntie. Her presence at home was not a surprise to me. I knew that she often visited the house in my absence, but left before I came home. Initially, many questions bothered me – why were there two coffee mugs in the sink, why was there an unusual floral scent that lingered around the house?

I eventually started to understand everything that had been going on between my father and her. In fact, everyone in my society knew. All this while, I had deliberately avoided playing with the other kids in the vicinity to avoid any questions. So much so, I purposely avoided an encounter with my father too.

I had known Soha auntie since I was a child. Whenever I needed any medical consultation, my father would take me to Noor Clinic. As a doctor, she was overtly caring and loving. It felt as if the clinic belonged to us. I started bringing my friends and everyone who needed a doctor to her clinic, and she never charged anything from us. I clearly remember how upset my mom was when she got to know that I had gone to the clinic with my best friend, Gagan.

I innocently explained that Soha auntie was kind-hearted and helpful, and that she never charged a single rupee from Gagan or me. She even offered candies every time we visited. But while I was busy boasting about Soha auntie's benevolence, my mom yelled, 'Don't you dare go to her clinic again.'

That roar was scary. I was only eight years old and I did not understand why she was getting so worked up about such a small thing.

Noor Clinic was the place where she was diagnosed with cancer. We had a series of tours to various other hospitals. I remember how we ran through major hospitals like Fortis, AIIMS and then finally settled for the last few days of my mom in Noor Clinic.

After my mother's demise, Soha auntie started coming to my house. It seemed like she was waiting for this to happen. She pampered me and always asked me about my well-being. Initially, I thought it was her caring nature, but later I realized she had a different equation with Papa. After all, an unmarried and decent-looking doctor has many things to offer.

My mom was truly an exceptional woman. I could never forget the day I had performed badly in my sixth standard maths exam.

My teacher refused to give my result card until my parents came to school. Gagan and I were the only ones whose parents were called. We understood that we were in trouble. Dad was struggling at his job end and I didn't want to disturb him at work, so I called my mom.

She was in the school office within half an hour of my call. Gagan's father was also there. Gagan and I were asked to stand outside while our parents met our teacher. All the teachers and classmates passing by gave us taunting looks. I had never felt so dejected in my life. I hung my head, staring at the floor. There was a heated discussion between our parents and the teacher. I tried to peek inside the classroom and wondered if my mother should have to face such humiliation because of me.

Suddenly I heard a voice. It was Rosy, a classmate who I had a huge crush on.

'Hey Anuj, how was your result?'

'It's maths!' I said without looking at her.

She came near me and touched my hand softly. 'Don't worry! I am with you.'

There was strange happiness on my face. I asked her, 'How was your result?'

'I got 90%,' she said casually.

'Oh! Good.'

Rosy then diverted her attention to Gagan.

'Hi Gagan! How are you? How was your result?'

'I am just giving company to Anuj,' Gagan lied.

'I think I failed in maths,' I said with a gloomy face.

She hugged me as consolation, and with her touch, millions of testosterones sparked inside my body. Gagan looked at me with disgust.

'Don't worry, it will be fine,' said Rosy.

'I think I also failed in maths,' Gagan said instantly, but to my joyous heart, he only received a sympathetic smile and nothing more. Gagan's round face was about to explode in jealousy. But then, his father came out roaring with anger, *'Oye, ye le naak katwa di tune.* You've made a joke out of all of us.'

Gagan had failed in three subjects and his father was really angry. He also gave me a disdainful look. It seemed he blamed me for everything bad that had happened with Gagan. The millions of testosterones floating inside me died out at that very moment.

My mom appeared and wished Gagan good luck as he was dragged away by his father. I was ready for my share of humiliation and unwanted *gyaan*. I almost closed my eyes, getting ready for the worst. However, nothing of that sort happened, and there was absolute silence for a few seconds. I opened my eyes and saw Mom standing there with a smile, holding my report card in her hands. She tousled my hair. Her smile confused me, but I was too scared to question her.

She smiled and asked, 'Why are you so scared, beta?'

'How is my result?' I asked in a low voice.

'Your result is good.'

'Really?' There was a smile on my face. I almost snatched my report card.

'No, let your Papa also see this.'

Suddenly, my face beamed with pride. I was amazed. I walked with confidence. When I reached home, I was curious to see the result. I looked at the report card and there was a big red circle over my maths marks with a remark in the ugliest handwriting I had ever seen – passed with grace. I read it thrice to be sure.

'Mom, you lied. I failed in maths.'

'No, you did not fail. You passed with grace.'

'But I disappointed you, Mom.'

I was almost in tears, but even before a single tear could flow out, my mom hugged me and said, 'Son, you have scored less in maths in class sixth, and it is a sign of being a genius.'

I freed myself from her embrace and gave her a strange look.

'Your father had also failed in the class sixth, your mamiji also failed in class sixth and Soha auntie also failed in class sixth.'

Surprisingly, I felt pleased at others' failures. Despite mourning over my bad performance, I felt like we all were the same kind of sinners.

Still, I was not convinced about how everyone had failed in maths in the same class. I was juvenile, but then I got calls from mamiji and mausiji and everyone confirmed that they too had failed. The same night, Mom gave me a handwritten greeting card. She was an expert in making cards. She used to make greeting cards on everyone's birthday. I opened the card and saw a message inside: "Congratulations on not doing good, but being a genius".

That night, before dozing off, I hugged my mom and asked her curiously, 'Are we a failed family, Mom?'

My mom hugged me and ran her hand through my hair. 'We are not a failed family,' she said calmly.

'Then?'

'Almost everybody in our family is weak in maths, but we do not cry when we fail. We accept and celebrate it and work hard for next year. It's okay to be average or to fail in an exam, but one should know how to recover from it. That is what our family is best at.'

'Thanks, Mom. I got it. Next time, I will top in maths.'

'No Anuj, you don't need to top in anything. Getting on top is not essential. Sometimes giving your best is the right way to go.'

This had happened so many years ago, and now, I had topped in my exams by giving it my best shot.

When I returned from school that day, Soha auntie was there. She always had a confident look on her face, but that day, it was missing. I wished I had called Papa before coming home. I went to the washroom and couldn't hold myself from crying. I was suddenly missing my mom.

I wanted to hug her and tell her that not only did I give everything my best shot, but also topped in my exams. I wanted to tell her that she had made me what I am today. I looked at my result and cried silently and when I came out of the washroom, I found Papa standing right outside the door.

3

Roshan

'Did you speak to Anuj?' Soha asked.

I did not reply, but she understood my silence.

'How is your clinic going?' I asked her, changing the subject.

'Nothing great happening. I have appointed a new manager and she is efficient enough to manage all the routines of the clinic. I only get involved in critical cases.'

'That's good. You can't do everything on your own; you need someone to help.'

'But that is draining all my earnings too,' she said with a sigh.

'But it would lessen your workload.'

She nodded. 'When will Anuj be back?'

'He went out to buy something... should be back any moment.'

'Then why did you call me now? You know it would not be a pleasant situation for both of us,' she said, glaring at me.

Our eyes met and she let out the breath she had been holding. She settled on the sofa and asked me, 'Would you like to have some coffee?'

I nodded. She moved towards the kitchen and shouted, 'Why is the kitchen so dirty?'

I smiled. At least someone was still there to shout at me. Her authority over me had never lessened. I walked into the kitchen where Soha was mixing coffee and cream.

Apart from Alka, our house cleaner, Soha was the only one who used the kitchen often. She knew every corner of it perfectly – coffee and milk powder, our stacks of cutlery and even the groceries. It was hard to believe that she was the owner of a clinic and a leading gynaecologist in the area. She never cancelled any appointments and personally replied to all her patients' queries, at the same time being strict about her "no messaging after 10 p.m." policy. It was compulsory for the clinic staff to be at the clinic by 8 a.m. She was a disciplined lady, but now, standing in my kitchen, she looked like an absolute opposite.

'Why are you staring at me like that?'

'Nothing, the kitchen always reminds me of many things.' I smiled.

She smiled for a moment. It was hard to imagine her as an outsider. She seemed just as much a part of this house as me and Anuj.

'Shall I talk to Anuj?' she asked, bringing me back to the scary situation we were in.

'You think it's a good idea?'

'It is not about a good or a bad idea. It'll mean we are trying.'

Soha radiated happiness, but she always questioned things around her. What are you doing? Why are you doing this? Is there a better way? She wasn't afraid to say her opinions out loud and also to make things happen her way, even if it meant fighting with the world.

We had our coffee in silence, entertaining the thoughts going on in our minds. Right then, there was a knock at the door.

'Hi Anuj!' I said opening the door. 'How was shopping?'

'I decided....' Anuj stopped mid-sentence as soon as he noticed Soha. He exhaled and looked at me with a million questions on his face. He did not say anything, just moved to his room. He did not even acknowledge Soha's presence.

Soha glanced at me, putting her hand on her chin unintentionally.

'He did not even say hi to you. Do you still want to talk to him?'

She nodded and got up.

'Alright, I will wait here.' I smiled, trying to instil some confidence in her.

'Anuj beta, this is Soha auntie.' She knocked, standing outside, even though the door was not locked.

Anuj did not respond, making me all the more worried.

'Anuj, we want to talk.' Soha tried again.

'Regarding what?' he asked opening the door

'Beta...'

'Excuse me,' Anuj interrupted. 'I have a small request, Soha ji. If possible, please do not address me as beta. Call me Anuj!'

Nobody had ever spoken to Soha in this tone. I wanted to end the whole conversation there and then.

'I am so sorry... Anuj,' Soha said.

'It's okay. You wanted to say something?'

'Yes, I do, but I guess you already know what I want to say.'

'And I am also sure that you already know my decision,' Anuj replied in a slightly raised voice.

'Yes, I can sense it.'

There were a few seconds of silence and I understood that the conversation had died even before it could start.

'Take care, Anuj. We respect your decision,' she said meekly.

'Wait, Soha ji! I wanted to ask you something. I hope you don't mind.'

'Yes, Anuj?'

'Why didn't you get married?'

'That is something personal.'

'Well, we are discussing something personal, right?'

'I can tell you the truth, but I guess you are not in the right frame of mind to understand.'

'I will never be in the right frame of mind for your answer, so please...'

She took a pause and continued calmly, 'To be honest, I focused on my work and studies and knew that our match was impossible. My family kept pushing me to get married, and when I finally decided to move ahead in life, I was already thirty-six years old. Then one day, your mother walked into my clinic with a deadly infection.'

There was absolute silence in the room. I was amazed at how Soha was holding fort so steadily when Anuj was evidently irate.

'So? From that moment on, you were waiting for my mother to die?' Anuj's voice cracked.

She stared at her feet silently.

'May I know the answer please?' he asked again.

'I don't know.'

'Really?'

'Before you judge me, Anuj, know that I have never had any thoughts against your mother. I did have feelings for your father, but I knew he had a family and respected that space.'

'Let us stop it here, Soha ji.'

'Sorry to have upset you,' Soha said without looking at Anuj.

'Why are you pretending to be so nice?' Anuj asked her. This was spiralling out of control.

'I am not pretending anything.'

'What is the use of asking about my decision when you know how I feel about it? At the end of the day, you guys would do whatever you feel like anyway. So why bother trying to be nice?'

'It is not about us. It was never about us. It is about all of us as a family, and your decision matters, son,'

'Then you know my decision.' With that, Anuj banged his door shut.

Soha gazed at me, took a deep breath and said, 'Roshan, could you please come with me to the clinic? We need to talk.'

I nodded. We drove to the clinic in her car, which was barely a couple of kilometres from my place.

She was silent through the entire journey and only looked at me thrice. It was almost noon, so traffic was not an issue. She was breathing hard and I tried to ask a few things, but I knew she was fighting an internal battle. She parked the vehicle outside the clinic.

Seconds after she entered her cabin, her staff started rushing in and out, briefing her about the daily operations of the clinic and giving her status reports of the patients. She signalled that she would talk about all that later. I was a frequent visitor to her clinic, so everyone knew me. It was hard to believe that she was the same lady who was facing Anuj a moment ago and was on the verge of breaking. She kept herself calm.

I looked around her cabin, which reminded me of a lot of good and bad memories. On the wall behind her were two framed certificates. One was the official clinic registration certificate and the other was her degree. Along with it were a few pictures of her, receiving awards, and one newspaper cutting showcasing her success.

I looked at all these things with numerous questions hovering in my mind. Did she really wait for me all these years? Had she waited for my wife to die? What was the need to bring it up with Anuj. Only a person like her could speak her heart out so bravely.

'We need to talk, Roshan.'

'Yes, Soha. I presumed the same, but now I am scared.'

'Why are you scared?' she looked at me intently.

'Because of your silence.'

She folded her hands and stared at me. 'I need a promise, Roshan.'

'Anything you say.'

'I think we should limit our meetings. Anuj is upset and I don't want to add to his woes.'

'I know. His anger is understandable,' was all I could say.

Soha went quiet after that and I knew she had something else going on in her mind. I insisted for her to share it with me.

'You need to try and convince Anuj about us. If he agrees to accept us, fine. Or else, I think we should end this relationship.'

'Do you know what you are saying, Soha?'

'I am a gynaecologist, Roshan. I have seen thousands of families and their love for children. One of the best things we could have in our life is our family. And I cannot spoil yours.'

This was not happening for the first time. Everything was replaying as it had years back. It seemed, nothing had really changed.

'What about us?'

'It is not about us. It was always about family. If he does not agree, then please avoid meeting me,' she said in her no-nonsense voice.

Now, there was anger raging in me. How could she give up so easily? 'Is that so easy for you?'

'I am forty-four years old and still unmarried, Roshan. Do you think it is easy?'

'Then why are you giving up on us?'

'I'm not giving up; I am asking you to try harder. And, we cannot raise a pyramid of our dreams when our child is pained by it.'

'That's alright. But what about us? Don't we have a life? I have spent my entire life struggling. When things finally started to settle, I got to know my wife had cancer. And now... this...'

'Why don't you understand my point, Roshan? I'm not saying let's end everything. Why don't you try to convince him?'

'I cannot do it alone.'

'You will have my support.'

'You don't understand my point, Soha. It is not about my wife or getting remarried. It is not even about you.'

'Then what is it about, Roshan?'

I looked at her in the eye. 'It is about his mother, and no one can take his mother's place.'

4
Anuj

Initially, I thought my father was attracted to Soha, but when she tried to talk to me, I knew their relationship was much beyond that. I understood what she was trying to do. I had never behaved like that with her before, because I had always seen her helping my family. Her goodness as a doctor was known to everyone, but now I understood why she never charged anything from me or my family.

I looked at the photograph of my mother I had in my room. She was smiling in the photo, something that I will never be able to see, except in this photograph.

I came to the drawing room and found two empty coffee cups on the table. My eyes landed on a big photo frame that held a picture of our family. Me, my father and Mom. We three looked like a perfect family.

My father seemed to have left with Soha for her clinic. I was all alone in the house with just my memories. I changed my clothes and while reaching for my shoes, I found a pair of fancy women's sandals. It was obvious that they belonged to Soha. It angered me to see her belongings so casually placed in our house. I looked around at what used to be my home, but I felt suffocated. I concluded that I was not wanted here anymore. This was the home I was born in, cried in, played in and spent my life in. But today, it felt strange. I grabbed my mother's picture and started stuffing my things into a bag.

I picked up my phone and called up my best friend. 'Gagan, where are you?'

'I am at home. What happened?' he said casually.

'Can you please come to my home, right now?'

'Is uncle at home?'

'No.'

'Reaching in a bit.'

Gagan was my childhood friend. I did not know how, but he somehow made time for everyone. I was almost done with my packing, with only a few more things to collect. A few minutes later, there was a knock at the door. I hoped that it was not Papa.

I looked through the window and saw a guy in a white turban, intensely engaged in his phone while waiting for the door to open.

'Hi Gagan, thanks for coming,' I said opening the door.

'Oh, no worries. When will uncle be back?'

'No clue.'

'Awesome,' he was suddenly in party mood. He threw his small bag on the sofa and picked the TV remote. It was then that he saw my packed bags.

'Wow, is uncle going for a long vacation?'

'No...' before I could explain further, he switched on the TV and started browsing through channels.

'Gagan, would you help me with the packing?'

There was no reply from him. He was glued to the TV.

'Gagan!' I shouted.

'Yes?' he finally looked at me.

'Put the remote down and help me pack my stuff.' I said with urgency.

'Why are *you* packing?'

'Because I am leaving this house.' I looked at him, waiting for a response. He stared at me open-mouthed. 'Before you ask anything, let me explain. I am moving to my maasi's place. My father wants to marry Soha and I obviously hate the idea.'

He was silent. He adjusted his turban and asked me with a confused look, 'So, why are you moving out?'

I flushed. It felt like everyone was out to test my patience.

'I am against the decision, so this is my way of reacting to their decision.'

'This is so sad.'

'I know. We cannot help it,' I said zipping up my second bag.

'This is very sad,' he said for the second time. I looked at him and realised he was busy doing something on his mobile.

I ignored and continued with my packing.

'Oh no!' Gagan suddenly shouted and took me by surprise.

'What happened?'

'Simran blocked me on Facebook. Does your maasi have WiFi at her house?'

'What?' I shook my head and ignored him, signalling him to help me pack.

'You called me to pack your stuff?'

'Yeah. So?'

'I thought your father was not here, so we will watch a movie together and I even came with a pen drive with movies on it.'

'Are you crazy? Here I am, struggling with my life, and you are worried about friend requests and movies?'

He made a face as if I had stolen his right to vote. 'By the way, what is the problem if your father likes Soha auntie? Even I like her.'

'I don't know if you heard me or not, but my father wants to *marry* her.'

'That's cool! You will have a new mummy.'

I wish he had some manners. Or maybe a filter on his tongue. I gave him a sideways look which spoke of my frustration.

'What? Why are you looking at me like that? Did I say something wrong?'

I opened my mouth to shout at him, but his phone suddenly beeped and his attention quickly diverted to his phone. He was suddenly screaming and dancing in joy.

Simran had accepted his friend request.

5
Roshan

I came back from the clinic, angry, confused and worried. Anuj opened the door avoiding any eye contact with me. He was dressed in a black T-shirt, jeans and sneakers. It looked like he was going out somewhere.

I sat on the sofa and looked around. I wondered why it felt so different. Something was missing. Oh! Anuj's books were not on their usual shelf anymore. His favourite trophy was also gone. Panic started setting in, and I went into Anuj's room to calm down my fears. My wife's photograph was not on the wall anymore. Before I could register anything, my gaze landed on Gagan.

'Namaste Uncle ji.'

I nodded in response and walked towards the lobby. I found three big bags at the corner of the room. Anuj zipped closed a bag. I chose to stay quiet and came back to sit on the sofa. This shouldn't be happening, my heart screamed. I had flashes of multiple images – the time when Anuj was born, how we clicked millions of pictures with him, how I narrated stories at night, how he walked along with me in every struggle of life, how I used to save him from Manisha whenever he landed in trouble as a child.

Anuj appeared with three bulky bags. He was clearly not the small child anymore, who used to hold my hand. He had grown up... enough to pack up his bags and leave unannounced.

'Papa, I am going to Alisha maasi's place for a few days.'

'Are you sure you are going for a few days? Seems like you are shifting permanently,' I said looking at his bags.

'No, I will be back soon.'

I did not know what to say. 'I wish you could have waited till your birthday.'

He ignored my request and got busy booking a cab on his mobile.

'Shall I drop you somewhere?'

'No, Gagan will help me out.'

'So, he knows everything?' I asked. He nodded.

'The cab is here, Gagan. Let's go!'

Anuj was already moving out of the house before I could say anything. I wanted to stop him, but all this happened in a flash. I realized that he had made up his mind and words couldn't help now.

I picked one of his bags to help him, and Anuj resisted. I ignored him and helped him load his bags in the car. Gagan was looking at me with subtle sympathy, which I did not like at all. I looked at Anuj and noticed that he had tears in his eyes. I knew he wanted to say something.

'Bye Papa,' was all he said before he moved inside the car. In that one moment, it felt like I was losing my son.

'Can I at least get a hug?' I said in a cracking voice.

He came out and gave me a quick hug.

'Can't you tell me what the problem is? Is it important to leave like this?' I whispered.

He had a look of disbelief on his face. 'A Muslim woman cannot replace my mother,' he said in a firm tone.

'What if she was not a Muslim?'

'Take care, Papa." He got inside the car, trying not to look at me. I knew he was trying hard to hide his tears.

6

Anuj

Gagan and I were heading towards Alisha maasi's place. Her place was like a second home to me. Gagan had already been to her place many times, so she knew him well. The summer heat, the humidity and my displeasure were at its peak, but it didn't seem to bother anybody else as much as it bothered me. Everywhere I looked, I could see crowds.

Gagan was trying to make some conversation with me, but I was stubbornly staring in the opposite direction. Failing to grab my attention, Gagan diverted his focus on our cab driver.

'Bhaiya, which is better? Ola or Uber cabs?'

The driver, who perhaps was waiting for someone to start talking, started telling him the benefits of both Ola and Uber in detail. Soon enough, Gagan and the driver were so engrossed in the conversation, I felt both would leave this cab as business partners.

I was busy staring out of the window, when my phone vibrated. It was a new WhatsApp message. One of my friends had forwarded some link with a news piece, titled: *Hindu religion is in danger*. I clicked on the link to read the whole article.

Union Home Ministry raised concern over mass conversions in the country.

Hindu religion is in danger: The relative growth of Muslims in Assam during 2001-11 has been extraordinarily high. The share of Muslims in the population of the state has risen by 3.3% in this decade. This is the highest accretion in the Muslim share for any state; the average accretion for India has been only 0.8 %.

This is also the highest accretion in the share of Muslims witnessed in Assam in any decade since Independence.

I read the message and my mood turned worse. Hate and revenge have the power to induce a strange kind of energy in humans. I was already feeling dead on the inside for the last few minutes, and now, I was ready to pick up a fight with anyone.

I am sure the same feelings had started reflecting on my face. Gagan took the phone from my hand to check what had agitated me now.

'Why do you hate Muslims?' he asked.

'Are you a fool? Do you really need me to start telling you the reasons?'

'Yes.'

'Can't you see why all terrorists are Muslims? Why all Muslim-populated places in India – especially Kashmir, Assam and Bengal – are turning into Muslim majority states? That is because they convert. They do not respect other religions. According to them, there is only one religion, which they keep propagating by hook or by crook.'

'How can you be so sure?' Gagan asked matter-of-factly.

'Do you know about Bali?' I asked Gagan, who looked clueless.

'Yes, it's a Hindu country.'

"It's not a Hindu country, but one Hindu city in a Muslim-dominated country, Indonesia. Wait...' I quickly opened a WhatsApp group and showed Gagan another message which read:

Are Hindus in danger?

Why does Indonesia have a huge Muslim population, despite a history of hundreds of years under Hindu and Buddhist kings?

The answer to the question is simple: Because Islamic teachings encourage proselytizing religions. Hindus and Buddhist don't generally convert.

'From where are you getting such valuable knowledge? WhatsApp university?' I understood the sarcastic tone in Gagan's question.

I did not like how he was mocking me with his words. 'No! I have verified all this information from Google and other websites.'

'But Christians also do conversions, and they also believe in one god. Why target only Muslims?'

'Let me show you!' I did not want to give up so easily.

I typed "Five pillars of Islam" into Google and showed Gagan the results.

The five pillars of Islam are five basic rules in Islam that all Muslims should follow:

1. The Shahadah: which means that there is no other god except Allah (one god) and Prophet Muhammad is the messenger/prophet of Allah. The line can be recited when a person chooses to convert to Islam as the words in the shahadah are the key fundamental beliefs in Islam.

'See this,' I said pointing at the passage that read, 'There is no other god except Allah.'

'So? What is wrong in that?'

'What about the other religions and their god?'

He read that line a few times and said, 'But these lines are for a Muslim to follow, right? Why would a Muslim need to believe in some other god?'

7

Roshan

I had failed to give Anuj the comfort to open up to me, or perhaps I had never understood him. I kept asking myself whether I was doing the right thing. Soha had asked me this so many times and I was sure. Honestly, I didn't think I was doing anything wrong by choosing to follow my heart, but I also did not know why I had never got any support in this particular decision. I still remember how I met Soha for the first time.

My father owned a huge two-storied stationery shop, right next to Noor Clinic in Rohini, Sector 16. The Noor Clinic was about double the size in comparison to our shop. Back then, it was owned by Dr Khan, who was a leading general surgeon and a respectable man in our area. I had never heard anyone call him by his actual name. He was popular as Dr Khan.

I stood in the stationery shop, surrounded by all the glittering and shimmering gifts, greeting cards and wrapping papers, when I heard a soft voice calling for my father.

'Uncle, do you have a white chart paper?'

The voice belonged to the prettiest girl I had ever seen. Although I was just ten years old and hadn't had many interactions with girls, this was the first time I was genuinely dumbstruck. I wasn't interested in any of the shimmering things in the shop anymore. I was more in awe of the little girl who had walked into our shop.

'What is your name?' my father asked her.

'Soha.'

My father nodded in response, rolled a big white chart paper and handed it over to her after securing it with a rubber band.

She seemed to be around my age and wore a cream-coloured frock. I had never seen somebody's pigtails as exciting as hers. As she swayed with playful enthusiasm, her long, thick pigtails seemed to be dancing and swaying along with her. I couldn't stop staring at this astounding phenomenon.

'How much?' she asked.

'This is free for you,' my father replied with a huge smile, which made her smile too.

She was delighted, but did not even say thanks. Wasn't that the basic thing to be done? Suddenly, the cute girl started looking rude and evil to me.

'Papa, why didn't you charge anything for the chart?'

'She is our neighbour, Dr Khan's daughter.'

'So? Do neighbours get to have things for free?'

'No.'

'Then?'

'Sometimes, the relationship is more important than business.' He closed the discussion and went about his usual work.

I did not understand what he meant, but I didn't like the way she was getting things from my shop for free.

She eventually became a regular at our store. Sometimes she asked for an eraser, sometimes a pencil and often notebooks. My displeasure was at its peak. Now the pretty girl appeared pure evil to me.

The school that I studied in was only till the fifth standard. We had to now look for another school for my further education. My father secured admission for me in Delhi Public School, which was an affluent one and way out of our financial league. I failed to understand how my family managed the school fee. I had occasionally caught my parents whispering a lot about the school fee, and the never-ending expenses that came with the admission. Every argument seemed to settle with a single line – he is our only son.

The school welcomed me with a series of instruction on the very first – day.

'Ask your parents to buy you a proper pair of white socks.'

'Tell your mother to iron your clothes from tomorrow.'

While this was scary in itself, to make matters worse, there was a sea of unwanted and unfamiliar faces that did not seem to be ready to accept me. But amidst all of them, there was one familiar face – Soha. She was still the unwanted neighbour who walked up to my shop and got things for free. There were a handful of girls in the class, and there was limited interaction between us, mostly during lunch.

I was struggling with a lot – many unknown faces, new curriculum and a new science syllabus, which was harder than ever. And then there were the compulsory moral science classes. I figured that moral science was more critical than any other classes combined. I was struggling hard to understand English and the whole new world that this school was. No one tried to make any conversation with me, like I was an outcast. I still needed to go a long way.

Sometimes I would catch the only known face looking at me. I guess she was trying to make a conversation with me or even trying to help me. Even though I always chose to ignore her, it was difficult to avoid her. We almost had the same route, she was always accompanied by her elder brother.

One day, a few months later, she came to me, offering her tiffin. 'This is for you, Roshan.'

I looked at her tiffin and saw some kind of a sweet dish. My face had a question mark.

'It's sheer khurma,' she said with a smile.

I shrugged, unable to understand what that meant.

'It was Eid yesterday.'

'I don't like sheer khurma," I replied harshly and gave the box back to her. I am sure my watering mouth was indicating the exact opposite.

'Who doesn't like sheer khurma? It is just like kheer,' she said.

'I don't like it.'

Her face drooped in sadness and I realised I did not like her cheerless face. 'Why are you sad?'

'You are not eating because I am a Muslim.'

Muslim? What a weird thing to say! Why would my refusing food have anything to do with that? And what is bad about being a Muslim. In fact, she had unintentionally made me realize that I was a Hindu.

I picked up the spoon and dug into the super delicious kheer, and then took another. Within a few minutes, I had finished half of that kheer. I did not know why that pleased her. But her happiness contented me as well.

That night I asked my mother, 'What is a Muslim, Mom?'

'What happened ...?'

'One Muslim girl offered me kheer today at school.'

My mom was suddenly shocked and her sudden change in mood surprised me. 'Muslims are bad. Do not have kheer from them ever again, son.'

'Why are Muslims bad, Mom?' I asked her with even more confusion.

'Because they are different ...'

'Are all different people bad?'

'What do you think?'

'They are good; they make good sweets.'

My mother smiled at my answer. Hunger and innocence make a person secular. My mind kept wondering all night whether being different meant being wrong.

On the school front, I was struggling hard with my new syllabus, trying to understand various terminologies. Everything was in English. My previous school was Hindi medium, and everything was taught in Hindi. Because of this abrupt change, nothing made any sense to me.

Soha did exceptionally well in every test. When the half-yearly results were announced, both Soha and I topped the exams. She became the topper of our class; I topped from the bottom. Her name always appeared as first, and mine as the last. Every day, my father would ask me to mingle with studious friends. I concluded, failure was a contagious disease.

Our maths unit test results were announced and I received 3 out of 30. My answer sheet was decorated with ten red circles, fifteen red underlines and a remark saying "Very poor handwriting". I scanned that for a few seconds and placed it silently inside my school bag. I thought I had been through enough humiliation in the class, but I was wrong. There was more to come.

Radha ma'am, our maths teacher had distributed all answer sheets, but had kept one with herself. After handing out the rest of the sheets, she announced in a euphoric voice, 'Guess who topped the unit test?'

'Sohhaaa...' half of the class shouted.

Jealously ran through my veins, but the trend seemed to continue in every other class.

One day, during lunch time, I went to her. She was busy eating her food and chatting with other girls. Without waiting for her to acknowledge my presence, I said, 'Friendship has no religion.'

She was shocked by my sudden arrival. She stared at me for a few seconds.

'What do you want? I have to finish my lunch.'

'Sorry,' I replied, suddenly embarrassed.

'I guess my timing was wrong.' I decided there was no point waiting to ease the conversation and asked her directly. 'Can I sit with you during lectures?'

'Why do you want to sit with me?'

'Because we are neighbours. My father's shop is just adjacent to your Abba's clinic.'

'So what if our parents are neighbours?'

'Why can't we?' Something in those words might have struck true with her, because from that day onwards, I shifted my seat next to her. I was the only one in our class who had broken the great barrier of sitting next to a girl.

Soha was a helpful girl. I noticed that almost everyone came up to her with doubts, seeking help. I was delighted that I had a greater advantage. Apart from getting all the academic help, I even got a big chunk of her delicious tiffin.

Eventually, we became best friends. Soha's brother had moved to Germany for higher studies and that allowed me to accompany her till home after school.

I still remember that one day when we were in the eighth standard. It was our moral science class with Miss Malini. She always had some illogical stories, which had nothing to do with science. Once she was narrating an extremely long and exhausting story and I had already yawned five times by then; my eyes were barely open when something she said made me more awake than ever. 'Hindu-Muslim bhai bhai.'

Suddenly, sleep vanished. I looked at Soha. She smiled. As if reading my thoughts, she replied, 'Don't worry, you are not my bhai.'

I did not know why, but that one line landed me on cloud nine.

⌘

Every day Soha had something interesting to share. Sometimes it was related to Allah, other times it was facts related to Germany that she had learned from her brother. As time went by, I understood many things related to Allah. I was a good listener, but I later realized that people classified me as an introvert instead.

Eventually, she topped in class tenth and that was the toughest year for us. Soha opted for biology and I realized science was too difficult to survive, so I opted for humanities. I was genuinely happy for her and wanted to gift her something. I tried to pick some money from the shop, but failed. My eyes landed on some fancy-looking key rings. I picked up a few and found the perfect one – a key ring that read, 'A born winner'.

I picked the best and the most sparkling wrapping paper I could find and gift-wrapped the keychain. I added a note to the packing that read, 'To a winner, from an outstanding loser.'

It was a small box, so I could perfectly hide it inside my pocket. I wandered the entire day in school, with the gift in my pocket, wondering how and when to gift it to her. The entire school was congratulating her over the success and I felt I was unwanted. I decided not to give her my gift at all.

On the way back home, she suddenly stopped and asked me, 'What are you hiding in your pocket?'

'Oh, how did you know? I got something for you,' I said sheepishly.

'I had noticed it in the morning itself. Show me, what is it?'

I handed it over to her, saying, 'This is for you.'

She excitedly tore away the wrapping paper, letting the card go unnoticed.

'This is so beautiful. Thank you.' I was delighted to see her smile.

Then she noticed the card and looked at me. 'You are not a loser,' she said with a wave of slight anger shadowing her face.

'Come on! I just wrote it without thinking.'

'Never call yourself a loser.' She meant each word.

I went silent because of the conviction with which she was saying that. I tried to divert her attention to other trivial things, but her mind was stuck on the note. I pretended to be in a hurry to reach home to finish a pending task. She nodded and before I rushed back home, she hugged me and whispered, 'A winner is a loser who tries again and again.'

The classes now were tougher, because I was habitual of sitting next to Soha. Her absence was too much to handle. So we made a promise to have lunch together. Lunch became the best part of the day for me.

One day during our conversation which majorly revolved around careers, she suggested for the first time that I should become an advocate.

'Advocate?'

'Don't you know who is an advocate? Haven't you seen one in movies? The one who wears a black coat and screams his lungs out, shouting big dialogues?'

My perspective of Indian courts back then was all thanks to Bollywood. I thought they would be royal in appearance. A lavish table for judges, two guards to escort them to and from their desk, and a court full of people rooting for each side. All this led me to believe that Indian courts were nothing less than a grand palace.

I imagined myself wearing a black coat and standing in the middle of the courtroom, delivering my speech in a loud voice. I was starting to see the glamour in her idea. I did not know where she always got so much information from. She seemed to know about everything. On the contrary, I was usually surrounded by books at the shop and at home, but barely had any knowledge about anything.

Our friendship had grown stronger over the years, but at the same time, it had also grabbed unwanted attention and comments. I often accompanied her to the nearest Dargah on Fridays, for her namaaz. I tried not to be bothered by the rumours and unkind comments that followed. People often said I had no shame or that I was lustful, following a girl like that. Fortunately, Soha seemed to be unaffected too. But not for too long.

It was Sunday, 6 December 1992 and I was helping my father in the shop. We were in twelfth then. I noticed that the Noor Clinic board was missing from the building opposite us. There were a couple of people rushing in and out of the clinic in a hurry. I fathomed something was wrong. I wanted to check with Soha and know what was going on. It was only in the afternoon that I got the full wind of what was going on.

News of the demolition of Babri Masjid spread by noon on 6 December 1992. Muslims were deeply angered by this act and felt that Islam was in imminent danger. After all, proponents of the majorly Hindu nation had been allowed to do such a massive and brazen destruction, right under the nose of the armed forces, despite assurances and undertakings by the Uttar Pradesh state government. Schools, colleges and public offices were closed down for a few days.

On a tea shop, I had heard the radio announcing how people were dancing on the dome of the mosque. There were also video shots being shown on TV, showing the actual demolition of the Babri Masjid, which further caused a sense of deep resentment. The demolition of the mosque provided enough fuel to excite, ignite and exploit the sentiments of the Indian Muslims.

Rumours abounded that alleged members of certain Hindutva parties were seen to be celebrating the demolition of the Babri structure. The first targets of the rioting mob were the municipal vans and the constabulary, both visible representatives of the government.

My father ordered huge bundles of newspaper and our bookshop was making good money selling them. Newspapers were in huge demand and were selling at double the usual price. Heavy force was deployed on the roads. Days had passed, but nothing had been resolved. I was getting restless. It was the longest since I had not seen Soha.

I stood outside her place, but there was no movement inside her house. I sat at a tea stall and started observing her house. With the tense situation around the city, sitting in a suspicious scenario was even more dangerous. A few policemen caught me sitting there and asked me to head back home.

I spent the entire night wondering about Soha. Next day again, I stood outside her home and after half an hour of waiting, I noticed some movement in the house. Someone had lit a lamp for a few seconds and had snuffed it almost immediately. It assured me there was someone in the house.

I went closer to the house and knocked on the door with hesitation. No one replied. I knocked again, but heard nothing in response. After almost ten attempts in about twenty minutes, the door opened with a jerk.

'What?' Dr Khan asked irritated.

I failed to reply to him and he roared again, 'What do you want?'

'Nothing. I was wondering if you guys were safe.'

'Till now we are safe. Please don't come here again,' he said and closed the door.

The newspaper was flooded with hate messages in days to come. There was some section of people advocating that all Muslims should go to Pakistan. That it was a new Hindustan, land of Rama. Few even said that Muslims were a lower caste. On every chai stall, this stupid discussion rose higher and deadlier. We had lived with friends, neighbours, relatives and unknown people, but that incident had forced everyone to classify each other as a Hindu or a Muslim.

I was in the shop, helping Papa when I heard a familiar voice.

'Can I talk to Roshan?'

There, on the entrance to our shop, stood Soha. She was wearing an ivory-coloured kurta paired with a golden pyjama and a dupatta loosely wrapped around her head. She looked radiant and seemed to be glowing against the afternoon sun. Her hair played hide and seek under the dupatta, the peacock-shaped earrings that dangled and moved around with each word she spoke – were all a new sight for me. This was the first time that I had noticed her in that light. I was meeting her after sixteen days and six hours.

For a moment, I felt the world was such a beautiful place and there was nothing wrong with it. There was no Hindu, no Muslim... only love. My father looked at me. Before he could say anything, I was already outside, with her.

'Can we go somewhere and talk?' she asked me in a serious tone. I nodded and headed quickly to the nearest auto stand.

I hailed the first auto we saw and she instructed the auto driver to go to the Pitampura Park. I sat beside her and could not believe that she was the same girl who I had been dying to see all these days.

She was consciously avoiding any eye contact with me. Her silence was killing me. I tried to get her attention with a couple of questions, but she did not reply.

The auto dropped us outside the park a few minutes later. For a park right in the centre of a bustling city, it lacked any warmth or romantic charm. A few couples, mostly college students, wandered the park – hand in hand and hip to hip. Soha kept walking and I followed her, all kinds of thoughts running in my head. She took a seat at the corner bench under the shade of a big tree. It was the perfect spot for us as it provided both shade and privacy. Considering the scenario and her choice of seat, I couldn't help but drag my mind into some romantic scenes that could give all the Bollywood movies a run for their money.

'Why did you come to my house that day?' She paused the music playing in my head.

'I was worried about you. There were attacks happening against Muslims.'

'Why were you so worried about me?'

I wanted to say that it was because she was my best friend, but something stopped me.

'Because of you, I had a horrible fight with my father. He thought you came there because of something else. That is why I want to know. Why did you come, Roshan?'

'Because I love you, Soha.' And just like that, I had said such a crucial thing. There were no romantic songs, no fancy settings, and no one shooting or clapping for us. I just said what came to my mind.

'You know we are Muslims and you are...'

'I know what religions we practice, Soha,' I completed her sentence.

'Please don't come to meet me again, Roshan. Stay away from me. You don't understand what it means to be a Hindu or a Muslim, especially in a time like this.'

I looked around and saw a few couples hugging. I even saw someone sleeping under the tree. But nobody could see how cruelly my heart was torn at that moment. Soha stood up swiftly, grabbed her bag and looked at me. But I was too numb and upset to look at her. I kept staring at a tree in the opposite direction, as if it was teaching me valuable life lessons and was way too important to be missed. Even if it meant Soha was walking away from me. My best friend and the only girl I ever cared about, was walking away. Suddenly it hit me that I was letting Soha walk out of my life. I would lose her forever.

I ran after her and caught up with her just outside the park, getting into an auto. Without even thinking, I jumped into the same auto, shocking both Soha and the driver. I expected Soha to yell or push me out, but all she did was tell the driver our destination. Then it was all silence.

Just as we were about to reach our neighbourhood, I said, 'Sorry if I hurt you.' But all I got in response was a gentle nod.

When we reached, she took a long breath and said, 'My parents love me and sometimes we have to put others before us, even if we don't want to. It's not always about us. Our exams are near. I hope you will focus on that. Study well and please don't come to meet me again.'

I nodded.

'My family is everything to me,' she sighed.

'And what about us?'

'Please understand, Roshan. We can live without a religion; we cannot survive without our family.'

8
Roshan

The final board exams for the twelfth standard were about to begin in a few days. After that rendezvous with Soha, I had diverted all my attention and energy onto the exams. Clearing board exams wasn't an easy task, so I put in more effort. I continued to miss Soha, though.

Like every other student, I used to resort to prayers during the exams, and become religious overnight. Eventually, I realized god was not helping me, so I decreased my prayers. But ironically, my parents increased their quota of prayers after each exam I wrote. To my surprise, my parents' prayers were answered and I did decently well in my exams.

School had officially ended, and it was impossible to meet Soha. I used to see Soha going in and out of her father's clinic, but she never looked at the shop. I think sometimes when we find love, we push it away, or choose to ignore it. I used to hope for Soha's slightest glance or attention towards me, but it didn't happen. Seldom, if I was lucky, I used to catch her looking at me. She would quickly divert her gaze, making me think that I must have imagined it.

If this turmoil wasn't enough, my results were out. The percentage was giving my father panic attacks.

'How will you get college admission with these marks?'

'You know we can't afford a donation, right?'

'Why couldn't you have studied a little more?'

'How does everybody else get marks?'

Just when I was wondering about Soha's result, Dr Khan came rejoicing and aggravating my dad's disappointment in me.

'Soha has again topped her class. She topped the twelfth exams,' Dr Khan said while offering sweets to my father. My father took one with a polite smile, but I knew that lava was boiling inside him. I was going to witness its eruption after Dr Khan left. I too picked a piece of sweet from the box and tried to savour it while I was still alive.

Soha's success was killing my father. She was featured in our local newspaper which had published her picture along with a small interview. The interview mentioned that Soha was looking forward to pursuing MBBS. I had read the interview thrice, and not satisfied with that, I had even cut out the whole interview and saved it inside my wallet.

The interview was a reminder to me that she was too high for me to reach. I stopped looking at the clinic and decided to follow a different path in life. I joined Karori Lal Law College to chase the dream that was handed to me by Soha. She may not have thought that I would be seriously following her words, but I had decided that I would become a lawyer.

The beauty of law colleges in our country is that it is more or less like a self-study centre. Professors came and went like wind and touching upon an entire year's worth of curriculum in a single lecture. This also meant I had a lot of free time. Moreover, all the humiliation and failures of my life were making me negative.

One day, I was sitting at the shop counter when a lady dressed in a burkha walked to my shop. I looked at those eyes and couldn't stop feeling a sense of familiarity. There was something captive about those eyes. Just as I was about to open my mouth, my father came barging into the shop, shouting my name.

Almost suddenly, it hit me that the lady in the burkha was none other than Soha. But before I could say anything, she ran off to the clinic. I followed her. I stepped into the clinic and followed her inside Dr Khan's cabin, which was empty. Soha removed the cover from her face and offered me a chair. There was a storm raging inside me. I had survived these days in the worst way possible. From talking all the time to not talking to her at all had been a disturbing shift for me. I missed the fun we used to have together. I missed our talks. I missed her.

'Where is your father?' I asked while relaxing on the chair.

'He has gone to Meerut for some work and will be back by tomorrow.' She didn't look pleased at all.

'Congratulations, you topped in school.'

'Thank you.' Soha looked at me. 'Why did you not come to meet me?'

I did not understand what she was trying to say. She was the one who had requested me to not meet or talk to her. We may be the masters of our thoughts, but we are also slaves to our emotions.

'I was ecstatic when I topped in school and my happiness grew multi-fold when I saw my interview in the newspaper. My father, family, everyone was delighted to see my achievement and the union minister came to our house to appreciate my achievement. I got admission in medical college based on my grades. But even then, there was sadness in me. Do you know why? Because I wanted to share my happiness with my best friend. I was so exhilarated in the beginning, but I realized I have no friends to share the happiness with. I have no one who would tease me, who would ask for a fancy treat. My best friend with whom I had shared all my happiness was not even bothered about my achievements. Yesterday I made sheer khurma, and I don't know why, but the sight of it made me cry.' She finished the sentence in tears. Then she gathered herself and added, 'I am leaving for my college in Chandigarh tomorrow and I didn't want to leave without seeing you.'

She walked towards me and I could see that her eyes were filled with tears. I stood up from my seat and hugged her. For the first time, she whispered in my ears, 'I love you, my best friend.'

9
Anuj

'What a pleasant surprise!' Alisha maasi screamed as soon as she opened the door. I touched her feet and hugged her. Gagan was dragging my heavy bags, so I took them from him and carried them inside the house.

Alisha maasi was the closest to a mother figure for me, but I lovingly called her auntie. It somehow did not make me miss Mom as much.

'Will you come tomorrow?' I turned around and asked Gagan when I saw him leaving.

He looked at Alisha maasi and asked, 'Is the WiFi working at your house?'

She nodded with a smile.

'See you tomorrow morning then, Anuj.'

Alisha maasi and I exchanged a look and laughed, as we bade goodbye to Gagan.

Alisha maasi and her husband owned a two-storey sprawling property in the plush green heritage zone of south Delhi. It was one of those homes that drew your attention instantly as you passed by.

The house was spacious and each room was massive, with all the modern amenities you could think of.

While her husband wasn't so enthusiastic about interiors, Alisha maasi had an impeccable taste. The interior of the house was a prime example of that. Each room was a fine mixture of both contemporary and vintage design elements. Every time I visited the house, I could explore a new piece added to her already beautiful house.

Alisha maasi's husband was an active politician and had recently been promoted to the position of a block head within the party. So my aunt had added a patriotic touch to the house now. She had a portrait of Shaheed Bhagat Singh along with Rajguru and Sukhdev hung in the drawing room. At one corner was the picture of Atal Behari Vajpayee giving a speech.

'You could have told me that you were coming,' maasi said as I settled on the grand L-shaped sofa.

'I thought I'd give you a surprise.'

'Really?' she looked at the three big bags that I had brought with me. 'Is everything alright?'

'Yes! You always ask me to stay for longer. So I thought I should spend a few weeks here before college begins. I will move back once college is about to start.'

She nodded, but I knew my answer hadn't convinced her at all.

Different people have different journeys for different reasons. But in the end, we are all connected. Sometimes it is through family or sometimes just as mere humans.

Alisha Saxena was a friend, a philosopher, motivator and my mother's only sibling. She was two years younger to my mom. She didn't like me calling her maasi, because she found it old-fashioned. My mom and maasi had lived different lives, but they were so close that they seemed more like friends than siblings. Their equation was way beyond my understanding, but it also made me wish I could have a sister like her.

I had loved her place since childhood. They did not have any kids, so both uncle and maasi treated me as their son, pampering me to the verge of spoiling me. Alisha maasi's husband worked as a politician for a leading party and also owned three liquor shops. People who knew him used to call him Vijay Mallya of South Extension.

Alisha maasi, on the other hand, was mostly a housewife, but active as hell on social media. She was a strong social influencer. She owned a popular food blog, which was flooded with rare culinary art. Interestingly, she never cooked everyday meals, but was a fine curator for interesting recipes and culinary art from across the globe. She had almost forty thousand followers.

Alisha auntie walked in with a big glass of orange juice and two bowls full of cookies and chips. She always fed me like I was coming from Sahara desert after months of starvation.

'No auntie, I can't eat all this. Just the juice is enough.'

'At least try it once, beta,' she said, offering me a cookie. 'These are Spanish cookies made with Netherland butter.' When I did not move, she picked another one and broke it from the middle. 'Then try this. It is from Karachi bakery.'

'From Pakistan?'

'No, from Hyderabad. It's a well-known brand.'

I took one bite and realized how I had wasted my entire life eating Parle G. I passed a satisfactory smile. I know she held unadulterated love for me in her heart. I could walk into their house anytime. Honestly speaking, after Mom passed away, I was more comfortable here than at my home.

The one thing I liked best about her place was that they always ate together. They looked like a perfect family. I had never once seen them shouting or even arguing. Sometimes I felt remorseful as to why they did not have their own children. They would have been great parents.

At dinner time, I felt overwhelmed with all the love and affection that they were showering on me. All of my favourite dishes were on the table. But at the same time, I couldn't stop thinking about Papa. It bothered me as to what he would be doing for his dinner. Then the thought of Soha invaded my brain and all worry changed into anger. It occurred to me that probably because I was out of their way now, she would be in our house, in our kitchen, cooking dinner for him and enjoying their time together.

'What happened? You didn't like the food? Any problem with the curry?' auntie prodded.

'No! Everything is perfect.'

'Are you worried about your father?' uncle asked.

I shook my head in denial, but I guess they must have read it on my face. And these thoughts suddenly killed my eating capacity. The food which was still in my mouth was getting hard to swallow and both of them looked at me with concern.

I added as an afterthought, 'I am not worried about my father. He is enjoying his life, and I am making the most of mine.' Auntie stared at me and I almost regretted saying this. But she didn't say anything about it.

'So what is the plan for your birthday?' I guessed she was trying to change the mood.

'Oh, nothing special.' Somehow I was not excited about my birthday.

Meanwhile, uncle had finished his dinner and moved to his room after wishing me good night.

Only auntie and I were left now.

'This house is always open to you, Anuj. After Manisha left, I had asked you so many times to move in with us, but you only come here for a week or two. And this time, you came unannounced, and that too with three heavy bags. You are so upset and distracted that you cannot even eat. Tell me Anuj, did you have a fight with your father?'

'I don't want to talk about him.'

'So I was right.' I did not answer.

'Can I ask you something?'

She nodded.

'How was my parents' relationship? I mean, did my mother ever complain about Papa?'

'Every couple has issues, but overall she was contended,' auntie said.

I gave it some thought and framed the question that had been haunting me. 'No, my question is, did Papa love Mom?'

Auntie's face suddenly clouded with doubt. 'Why are you asking such questions, Anuj? Why would you doubt your father?'

I couldn't take it anymore, and the dam burst open. 'Because all through my life, I have had a lot of respect for him. He was a busy man, but he was always there for me whenever I needed him. Whether it was school events and celebrations, or anything at all. He never scolded me for bad grades. He never spoke badly to me or Mom in public. He was always the silent kinds, you know. I often felt he had no feelings or emotions, and was merely doing his duty towards us like an obligation. But when Mom was diagnosed with cancer, he fought the battle like our hero. Like... like... we were a perfect family.' There was a lump in my throat and I took a while to calm down.

Auntie spoke after a few minutes of uncomfortable, loaded silence. 'Manisha never complained about anything, Anuj. She was always in her happy place with you and Roshan.'

'I don't understand how he started seeing someone else so suddenly then?'

'I understand, Anuj.'

'No, I don't think you do, auntie.' I didn't know how I could tell her all that.

She smiled and stroked my hair. 'I know she is a cunning rich lady.'

'Are you sure you know who I am talking about?'

'I know you are talking about Soha.'

10

Roshan

When Soha said she loved me, it was the most romantic moment of my life. I could never explain in words what those words meant to me, coming from her. There was no background music, no dancers or special effects, but for me, that memory beats the best of romantic scenes and settings from the world over.

I had lost all hopes of talking to Soha or seeing her ever again after she asked me to stay away. So it was nothing less than a miracle and I relived that moment over and over in my mind. But soon, my thoughts started waging a huge battle. She was destined for bigger things in life and I was merely dragging along. She had dreams and ambitions and was on her way to become a doctor and take on the legacy of her father. But what about me? My legacy was a book shop. Even if this wouldn't be a matter, in the long run, there was something that couldn't be overlooked. No matter how I felt or what I wanted, the reality was that she was a Muslim and I was a Hindu. We were two boats that were sailing parallel to each other.

The meeting of these two boats only meant a crash, which was sure to drown us both.

It was way past 11 p.m. and sleep was nowhere close to my eyes. So I decided to take a walk. It was peaceful and eerie. Except for the stray dogs, nobody was around and awake. But then, Delhi had always been a city that went to bed early. Plus, back then, the whole concept of nightlife was yet to be invented.

After walking a few metres, I ended up in front of a mosque. I did not know why, but for a moment, I stood there and took in the view. I had never seen a masjid at night. The moonlight played some magical charm on its silhouette and it was a sight that was worth a thousand photographs. I sat in its courtyard and let the sight seep in, while the cool night breeze calmed my thoughts. I got up to walk back home after a while, but my eyes fell on a line written on one of the masjid walls.

"There is no god except Allah."

I read that line again and again, and just like that, my fears came back with renewed vigour. My sleep was gone forever. It was like the universe itself was telling me that Soha and I would never be together.

In the meantime, Soha had moved to Chandigarh for her college. Unlike now, keeping in touch was the toughest job those days. Those were the days when the postman was more important than doctors or policemen. They played cupid to so many relationships. The only way I could stay in touch with Soha was through letters, and that too had to be sent through her friend who stayed in Delhi's JNU hostel. Soha used the pen name of Malini to write to me. This helped us maintain our privacy, without having to alter our relationship in any way.

These letters were our only way to stay connected and know what was happening in each other's lives. She shared about her experiences at the new medical college. She explained how she felt when she had to dissect a frog with her own hands, and how she ended up screaming during an open surgery on a mouse. She also shared how medical college was so different from what she had imagined.

My letters, on the other hand, not only had a description of events at my end, but were also thoroughly bathed in perfumes stolen from the shop. This was our version of a long-distance relationship. In those days I realised that missing someone gets easier with each day – even though you are days away from the last time you saw them, you are also one day closer to the next time you will be meeting them again.

With time, and the dying culture of reading books, with the invention of mobile and internet revolution, my father had to upgrade himself. The book shop was converted to a gift shop, which was good for me. I was able to pick whatever I wanted to gift Soha without burning a hole in my pocket. What all do we do for love!

She wrote so many letters in the beginning, but with time, the number decreased. From almost each weekend, the letters slackened to one in a month and eventually one in two months. Irrespective of that, I continued to write my heart out. I had finished my graduation from college and she was still pursuing her medical degree. I never demanded or complained about anything with Soha because I was pleased with the attention I was getting from her. I didn't want to do anything that could ruin this equation.

Around my twenty-third birthday, my father surprised me by asking me about the kind of girl I wanted as a wife. It scared me out of my wits.

'I am not ready for marriage, Papa,' I told him.

'I know why you are not ready.' My father's words were like a knife tearing through my heart.

The truth was visible to everyone and I did not dare to voice it out loud.

It was Diwali and Soha was home for the holidays. The Japanese garden, which was our regular meeting place, was flooded with flowers and beautiful paintings all around. The garden had fully absorbed the autumn spirit. While my mind was troubled with the thoughts of our future together, the park seemed cheery and blooming in beauty. On any other day, the view and atmosphere would have made me exultant, but that day, it was doing just the opposite.

It was a silent tour of the park for us. Soha was also unusually quiet and did not say anything much. Unable to take the silence, I decided to talk.

'My parents are looking for a bride,' I said hesitatingly.

'Oh, so it's finally the time!' She sighed.

'What does that mean?'

'You have already finished your education. I knew this was going to happen.'

'What about you?' I asked with a hope lingering in my heart.

'MBBS is two more years, and after that, a majors in Gynaecology. There is still time.'

'So your family is not pushing you for marriage?'

She shook her head in a no. I took her hand in mine and she clutched my hands in confidence. There was no worry on her face, but I did not see an expression of love too. All I could see was a strong determination. Like she was prepared for anything.

'Will you marry me?'

'Is that even a question?'

'Then what is?'

'I would only agree if my family agrees.'

'If your family doesn't agree, then?' I almost held my breath, waiting for her answer.

She looked at me with a look of disbelief, as if I was so self-centred to be even asking that question. I was confused, unsure whether I mattered to her at all.

'My family is my life; it is something Allah gifted me,' she finally said.

'Am I not gifted by Allah?'

'This is out of context.' She smiled.

'Shall I talk to your father?'

'I leave that decision to you.'

'Okay, but I would need your help.'

'I can't promise to fix all your problems, but I can promise that you won't have to face them alone.'

This was not the way I had hoped things to work out between us. She had offered me her support, but I still felt as if I was all alone in this battle.

'If you wish to talk to my father, talk to him on any Friday during Ramadan,' she added as a piece of advice.

'Why?'

'Because, during Ramzan, he practices *taqwa*.'

'What is taqwa?'

⌘

I had never been so courageous in my life. I did not know why I thought I could even talk to her parents. I looked at my face in the mirror and laughed inside. I asked myself, why should I be the one to talk to her father? After all, she also wanted to get married to me, so she should manage her side of the family. Why is she not ready to take on the wrath of her parents? Why am I being made the scapegoat? I would have dropped the idea of talking to Dr Khan, had it not been for a movie.

It was 1996 and *Dilwale Dulhania Le Jayenge* starring Shah Rukh Khan and Kajol had released. It had taken the nation by storm. I finally went for the movie, with my friend Mukesh, who was watching it for the third time. This turned out to be a bad idea because Mukesh kept narrating every scene before it even played. Even though I was irritated by his constant poking during the movie, the movie in itself indeed turned out to be good. Somehow my resolution to talk to Soha's father was back after watching the movie, especially after watching Shah Rukh Khan do all that to convince Kajol's dad. The movie had induced a new level of energy in me. I never thought a movie could inspire me so much.

I made up my mind the next morning and summoned all my courage by praying to all the gods I could think of. For a change, I also decided to pray to Soha's god. I knew, what makes us vulnerable, also makes us strong. I took a bus straight to Jama Masjid. It was a Ramadan Friday and I looked at the sea of people who crowded the place. I walked inside and stood at the corner and closed my eyes. I prayed for us for the first time and promised Allah not to ask for anything if he blessed me with Soha.

I even threw some tempting offers to visit Mecca Medina later. After hundreds of bribes and millions of pleadings, I opened my eyes and saw two people standing in front of me

'Are you a Hindu?' one of them asked.

I ignored them and started walking towards the exit, but they followed me and asked again, 'Are you a Hindu?'

'Yes! Are Hindus not allowed to pray to Allah?' I said and walked away fearlessly.

That gave me eccentric courage. I had already practised my dialogues about a hundred times on how I needed to deliver my case.

Being an aspiring advocate, I had never prepared for any case in such great detail. My hands were sweaty and my body temperature was rising in anticipation. If someone checked my blood pressure, I am sure they would have declared that I was about to burst.

I went to the Noor Clinic and asked for Dr Khan at the reception.

'Today is Friday. He may get late in reaching the clinic,' I was told politely.

'No issue. I will wait for him.'

'Don't you work at the stationery shop across the road?' the girl at the reception asked.

'I am the owner of the shop,' I said proudly. 'And it's a book shop cum gift gallery, not a stationery shop.'

'Okay!' The receptionist rolled her eyes, not at all impressed. 'You can leave, if you wish to. If the doctor comes, I will call you.'

'No, I will wait here.' I did not want my father to know what was happening, so I thought going to the shop was not a great idea.

I kept looking at the watch as minutes passed by sluggishly. I had used the washroom a good ten times in an hour. After almost two hours, Dr Khan appeared. He moved to his cabin and completely ignored me. I was called inside the cabin ten minutes later. I walked in with a racing heart and sat on the chair opposite him. I had a great memory with the cabin and this seat. It was the same place where Soha had hugged me and confessed her love for me.

'Aren't you the son of that bookseller?' he asked casually.

'Yes.'

'What can I do for you?'

I opened my mouth to speak, but suddenly there were no words. I was completely blank. I gulped some air and pretended to have something stuck in my throat. I pointed to a glass of water. Dr Khan nodded and offered the glass to me.

'Feel free to share your problem.' He was treating me as a patient.

'Uncle, I have heard that after the Friday namaaz, a true Muslim never denies a request.'

He nodded in affirmation. So far so good.

'I have come here with a request,' I paused to see his reaction.

'Could you come straight to the point? I am busy,' he said in a harsh voice.

'I like a Muslim girl and she also likes me.'

'Are you talking about Soha?' I couldn't read the expression on his face.

'Uncle, Soha loves me.'

I saw his face change. He passed a hooded look and his lips became narrow and thin. The vein in the middle of his forehead started to throb and he clenched his jaw. He was dead silent and closed his eyes tightly shut. It seemed he was praying. After a while, he stood from his seat and locked his cabin. Everything inside me was screaming for me to run, but I was too scared to even move from my seat.

Dr Khan came near me. 'Listen! I would only be ready if you accept Islam. If you understand that, you should leave.'

I never expected such a clear and straight response from him. I was amazed at such display of maturity and calm. Before I was leaving, he asked, 'You know about taqwa?'

I shook my head.

'Taqwa is a matter of the heart. The attentiveness felt inside the heart. A feeling that my lord almighty is watching me all the time. The realization that prevents a person from doing anything wrong....' So this was what Soha was talking about. I froze when he said, 'Taqwa saved you today.'

11

Roshan

As the world around us started getting modern and technologically advanced, so did we. We got home our first ever TV and Soha's hostel got a telephone. Delhi was also suddenly flooded with new public telephone booths. However, internet and smartphones were still years ahead and not even imaginable back then.

It had almost become a ritual for my father to have dinner with the night news bulletin which aired on the national channel, DD news. With time, we all became addicted to the news hour. On one such nightly routine, when we were having our dinner, one news piece came up that changed a lot.

Dawood Ibrahim Kaskar and Tiger Memon were identified as the main architects of the worst bloodbath India had ever seen. They were the prime accused in the Mumbai serial blasts case. As per sources, they were in Pakistan or somewhere in the gulf.

'How is it that all the terrorist are Muslims?' my father commented casually.

'Because Muslims don't consider India as their country,' my mother replied.

All I could think of while overhearing their discussion was – why all this couldn't have happened at some other time. All the doors seemed to be closing in on me and leaving me without any breathing space.

But I had to give it a try. 'Dr Khan is also a Muslim, but he helps people.'

My father passed a stern look, but continued to watch the news without saying anything.

It was clear that I would never be able to get my father on my side in this matter. Suddenly my dinner felt like a pebble stuck in my throat that refused to go down. On one hand, I wanted to be with Soha, but on the other, I didn't have what it took to convince both our parents.

My father said, just as I was about to go back to my room. 'A few days back, Dr Khan came to see me.' My mother frowned.

'He offered to purchase my shop... our shop, so that he can expand his clinic.'

'Isn't that a good thing?'

'If you were not so lost in your head and heart over his daughter, you would have easily seen that it is clearly not a good thing.'

My face was suddenly red. My head felt so heavy that I couldn't face my father.

'I don't understand why such a well-educated girl is interested in you. Is there any match between you and her?' my father said, and his words stung.

I stood there, looking at the floor. Also maybe because I knew he was speaking the truth.

'Don't you understand, Roshan? He is trying to involve you with his daughter so that he can have our land for free... and expand his business without paying a single paisa?' he spat the words in anger.

There were a million things that I wanted to say to him, about how Dr Khan was equally against the relationship. I wanted to tell him that the last thing Dr Khan wanted was me anywhere near Soha. But somewhere, my father's words still rang loud in my ears – 'Is there any match between you and her?'

⌘

Soha was supposed to come home for Eid holidays. She told me that her father had already imposed a lot of restrictions on her, even before she had actually reached there. I realised I had created so many struggles for her unintentionally. But restrictions were the mother of half of the innovations.

She had found a cyber café around our neighbourhood that provided individual cubicles for its users. The cabin was too small to accommodate two people. As we cramped together inside, my left leg touched the cabin's wall and the other was almost on Soha's lap. All my attention centred around our bodies touching. Soha, meanwhile, was busy doing something over the internet, while my mind was lost in her magical touch and smell.

'I have something for you,' Soha broke the silence, bringing me back to the matchbox-sized cubicle. She took out a box from her bag and gave it to me.

I took a few bites of the kheer immediately. It was heavenly, as always.

'How are your studies going?' I asked as soon as I could swallow the last bite of the delicious kheer.

'All good. I am planning for some rural internship.' I nodded my head in response.

'What happened? Why you are so silent?' she asked with a worried face.

'I met your father, Soha.'

'I know. What did he say? Was he rude?'

'No. He was nice to me. He was polite. He said he would agree to us, only if I agree to change my religion.'

She smiled.

'Why are you smiling at me like that?'

'He was not nice or anything, he just behaved politely because of Ramzan,' she said like she had cracked some secret code.

'Yeah, I know.' I smiled and we both started laughing.

I held her soft hands in mine and wished that this hand could belong to me for the rest of my life.

'Is there something bothering you, Roshan?' Soha asked most lovingly.

'Yes! We are poles apart, Soha. I have thought a lot, and I think we should end things here.'

She looked at our hands and said, 'So finally the time has come....'

I nodded, letting go of her hands.

'Don't be sad, my superhero!' she said.

'What hero?' I smirked

'I mean it; you are my real hero.'

'Enough, Soha! Don't make fun of me.'

She sighed and said, 'The day I accepted my feelings for you, I understood that we are different. I knew it would be impossible for both of us to get together, but I was amazed when you said you wanted to give it a try. It's an amazing feeling when someone tries, even after knowing what the result is going to be. Amidst all the confusion, I could only see your love for me.'

'Then why did you come into my life? If you knew it couldn't be, why did you accept my love?'

'I tried hard not to… but you know, we can live without religion, but not without affection.'

We hugged each other in that small space. There was a sweet fragrance around her, and a soothing warmth that calmed me down. We both were silent and had tears of hopelessness. Those few minutes were both the best and the worst for me.

12
Anuj

I sat in my room, wondering how Alisha maasi knew about Soha. I had tried to ask her, but every time I brought it up, she changed the topic. I realized that everyone knew about Soha already. I was the only idiot who had no clue about what was going on behind my back. The only thing I could learn from maasi was that my father's friendship with Soha went back to their childhood. Athough it did not come as a surprise to me, it did put me in a dilemma.

I did not want to think about it, so I tried to distract myself by playing games on my mobile or watching TV. But nothing worked. I clicked open the calendar on my phone and realized that I still had more than a month till college started. My eyes hovered over the date 8 June. I clicked on it and a small icon over there read "Your Birthday".

I wasn't excited about my birthday this year. In fact, I had not celebrated my birthday in the last four years. However, on my birthday last year, Papa had surprised me with a cake and had even called Gagan to celebrate. Now that I looked back, I realise that on that day too, Soha was there, sharing such a personal moment of ours.

The knock at the door broke my thoughts.

'It is open.' I assumed it would be Alisha maasi, but when the door opened, in came Gagan. He was smiling for no reason, like always.

'Hi bro! What's up?' He came and hopped onto my bed without even removing his shoes. It was hard to believe that a few seconds back he had been decent enough to knock on the door, asking for permission to enter the room.

'Could you please remove your shoes? This is not my house.'

'Then what are you doing here in this house?' he said while removing his shoes. Soon, a pungent smell engulfed the room. For a moment, I thought someone had leaked the nuclear reactor or something.

'What happened?' he asked me innocently.

'Can't you smell that?' I asked surprised that someone could have missed such a bomb.

'I have a cold,' he said and I exhaled a long-held breath. I knew it was futile to argue with Gagan.

'Please wear your shoes... it would be a great favour to humanity,'

He looked at me with puzzled eyes. He happily wore his shoes and passed me a wicked smile. I knew instantly that he did not have any cold.

'What happened bro? Why are you so upset with your father?' he asked.

I chose to not answer.

'What did Papa tell you that day, when you were at home?' I asked, suddenly remembering that my father had said something to him on the day I had left the house.

'That is something personal,' he said like he was hiding the greatest invention of a scientist.

'Gagan, can I ask you something?'

'Are you looking for advice?' Gagan asked with a smug smile.

'No, I don't need your advice. I just need an answer.'

'Okay.'

'Can a man love two people at the same time?'

His eyes popped out on my question. There was silence, which is quite unusual for Gagan. Looked like he was busy thinking and finding an answer. He looked at the ceiling and around the room for a while and then opened his wallet and pulled out two images. I thought he was missing his girlfriend. Then he said, 'Yes...'

'What do you mean by yes?' I asked still in shock

'I mean, I think a person can fall in love with two people.'

'How can you be so sure about that?'

He held up the two photographs and placed them on the bed in front of me. Then he said, 'Just look at them. Aren't they cute?'

'Who are they?'

'Simran and Jasmeet. I am in love with both of them.'

I sighed and looked at him. 'Gagan, there is a difference between love and lust.'

'I know that. I am serious about both the girls,' he said like my words had hurt him.

'Gagan, I am talking about my father.'

'What?' That got his attention. 'You mean uncle is in love with two aunties?'

I felt like strangling my best friend to death and burying him right there in that room. 'Never mind! Forget that I said anything.'

'So your father is in love with Soha?'

'Is this a valid question?'

He hesitated a bit and said, 'It's obvious. But the real question is, if your father loved Soha, then why did he marry your mom?'

13

Roshan

After that decision in the cyber café, we stopped writing to each other. There were no phone calls, no letters. We started avoiding each other; or to put it in a better way, we accepted reality.

My struggles started afresh from there. I joined as an assistant to a senior advocate named Mr Praveen Sharma. He was an independent practitioner and had almost half a dozen advocates working under him. He was one of those rare people from the advocate community who had a personal chamber in the court premises.

Initially, I was given the task of diverting any potential clients who came into court looking for an advocate towards Praveen Sharma. A good advocate is naturally a great salesman too. But they realized soon that they had appointed the wrong person for the task.

They changed my role to that of an office boy, running errands like doing photocopies and stamping the documents. A few months later, I was given the most tedious task of drafting and writing. I had always lacked in the writing department and drafting big things, so I naturally I failed at that too.

After changing my roles, multiple times, that too within a year, Mr Praveen finally took pity on me and gave me a final chance as his assistant. So my new tasks involved carrying his fat books and numerous unwanted files and always walking behind him. Initially, I thought he might require these heavy books and files, to refer during a discussion or debating about his client cases, but he never asked for any files I had been carrying. It took a while for me to understand that I was just his intelligent show-off. I kept carrying those bulky books tottering behind him for a few months, until one day, when he asked for a file. I had forgotten to carry it. Finally, I was asked to leave the firm.

I tried my hand at individual legal practice also. But as I said, an advocate has to be a good salesperson as well, which I was not, so even that did not work out for me.

One fine day, my mother ordered me to accompany her. 'Roshan! Get ready, we are going to the temple.'

'Why?' I asked, having lost faith in both, god and religions.

Before I could express my denial, my father came into the room and passed the verdict. 'Roshan, there is a purpose behind sending you to the temple.'

I didn't say anything. I could see that my father's eyes were already flooded with anger. I understood that any more delay in reaching the temple could harm me lethally.

I had assumed that my mother wanted to go the temple in our neighbourhood, but what she had in mind was the Birla temple – almost twenty kilometres from our house. The temple was located on Mandir Marg, towards the west of Connaught Place. The architecture of Birla temple spoke volumes about the time it was constructed in. It was built in the Nagaraj style of temple architecture with scenes from the golden yugas carved on the temple walls. The main temple was dedicated to Lord Vishnu and Goddess Lakshmi, with a huge hall that could accommodate hundreds of people. In fact, during the *aarti* in the morning and evening, the hall was brimming with people. It also had a side temple which was devoted to Lord Shiva. I sat on the marble floor, taking in all the sites, not wanting to go further.

'Mom you carry on, I am fine here.'

'What do you mean? You came to the temple and now you are denying to meet the lord?'

'No mom, I am not in the mood.' I was scared to face my father, but with mom, I was free and almost like an angry tiger. I looked straight into her eyes and said, 'You cannot force me to go inside the temple.'

She shrugged, refusing to indulge me further and moved towards the sanctum sanctorum, to pay her respect to Lakshmi-Narayan. Relieved and surprised, I went back to sitting on the floor at the entrance and taking in the sights around me.

After a while, I saw two girls dressed in white salwar kameez walking towards me. With both wearing the same kind of clothes, they looked like copies of each other. But as they neared, I could see that one was older than the other. The younger one seemed much chirpier compared to the older girl, who seemed to be a bit shy.

The younger one came to me and said, 'Are you Mr Roshan Dixit?'

I nodded.

She offered her hand. 'Hi, I am Alisha and this is my elder sister Manisha,' she said, motioning towards the elder girl.

Alisha was smiling for no reason and I looked at Manisha. She was holding something in her hand and was all coy and shy. In an instant, my father's words and my mother's sudden wish to come to the temple so far off made sense.

'Namaste, Manisha.'

I offered the politest response.

'Have you come alone?' Alisha was on another level of excitement. I guess everybody was excited, except me. Before I could answer, my mom made her entry.

'She is my mom,' I introduced my mother to them. Manisha touched my mother's feet and mom blessed her.

I understood that no one was going to ask my preference. I looked at Manisha, this time not as a stranger. I observed the way she was talking to mom and the way she smiled. I liked her. I knew it was just attraction. Standing there, I even did the cardinal sin of comparing Soha and Manisha.

Honestly, she was nowhere in comparison to Soha. I knew I was biased for her.

Suddenly there were chants and bells ringing. Mom took Alisha's hand and said, 'The aarti is about to start. Would you like to join me?'

Alisha joined her, and seeing my silence, Manisha too followed. All three of them went inside the temple. For a moment, I stood there baffled. Everything was happening so fast. I learned that courage was not the absence of fear, but the triumph over it.

I knew the aarti would finish in fifteen minutes. Which also meant that I had only fifteen minutes to make a wish. So I quickly rushed inside the temple and caught up with mom and Manisha. I went and stood next to Manisha. Before anyone could see us talking, I whispered to her, 'Can we talk in private?' She nodded in response.

After the aarti, my mother conveniently took Alisha to another side of the temple, on the pretext of showing her something. They were just giving us space and time to talk to each other. I grabbed the chance to talk my heart out.

'Do you know why we are meeting?' I initiated the discussion.

'Yes.' She gave me a smile. 'Do you wish to ask anything?'

'Yes, what do you do? Are you studying or working somewhere?'

'I am doing my degree in home science.'

Home science sounded like a different world to me. But home science meant that she would always be confined to home only.

'Manisha, I have an unusual request. Is it possible for you to say no to this match?' I asked in a muffled voice.

'Why?'

'I like another girl and I am scared to say no to my family.'

'Oh!' she groaned, 'Roshan, I need a strong reason to say no to the match. I am a girl and this is the fourth time I am meeting a boy. I am sorry, but you will have to take that call yourself.'

'You don't have a problem that I have another girl in my life?'

'We all live a different life, one before the wedding and one after we tie the knot. I have nothing to do with your past,' she said earnestly.

There was silence for a few seconds. Past, present and future – all started giving me goose bumps.

'Roshan, don't get me wrong, but I have something for you,' she said and offered me a greeting card.

'I cannot accept anything from you,' I said, embarrassed.

'Roshan, I made this on my own and spent the whole night creating it. So I hope you would at least take a look at it. If you still don't want it, I will take it back with me.'

I nodded and took the card from her, but hesitated to open the envelope. 'I guess I am not the right person for this.'

'It is just a friendly card. It is my hobby to make cards.'

I picked the card with a lot of appreciation. 'This is really beautiful,' I said taking a quick look at the card and putting it back into the envelope.

Just then, my mom came along with Alisha. We spent another hour in the temple and all the while, my mother treated Manisha like a hidden treasure she had been looking for, who was too valuable to part with. We returned home late in the evening.

The same night, lying on my bed, sleepless, I started wondering when all my struggles would end. Suddenly I was reminded of Manisha's card and I opened the beautiful handmade card which said,

> *To Roshan,*
> *Never lose a friendship because of a relationship.*
> *From,*
> *Manisha*

Before I could let that thought sink in, I saw my father standing at the door of my room.

'Hello advocate saab! How was the girl?'

'Which girl?'

He stared murderously into my eyes and fearing for my life, I babbled, 'I did not dislike her.'

I had added two negatives in one sentence. He spent a few seconds and concluded. 'Hmm, it means you like her.'

14
Anuj

I was taking a stroll in the Greater Kailash, M Block park, wondering about my upcoming eighteenth birthday. Gagan had turned eighteen last month, and he had thrown a party at a fancy place in Connaught Place. He had already asked thrice about my birthday plans.

I wondered what was so special about the eighteenth; it's just a number, after all. I checked my Facebook account and there was a notification which showed memories from five years back. I downloaded that image. I zoomed a little and saw my mother, my father and an innocent looking little me. I looked at my face for a few minutes and then my attention diverted to Papa. Despite what had happened between us in the past few days, it was edgy for me to hate him.

I returned to maasi's house and went directly to my room. The summer heat was making it hard for me to breathe. The AC in the room calmed my nerves, but only a bit.

Here, at maasi's place, all rooms were equipped with split ACs and a there was also a full-time servant to clean and serve great food throughout the day. Shifting my house from Rohini to South Extension was like upgrading from Indian railways to a flight.

There was a knock at the door. It was Alisha maasi. I smiled and told her, 'Auntie, you don't have to knock.'

'That's just good manners, my boy.' She returned my smile with a bigger one.

She looked great and I wondered, I had never seen my mom wearing jeans or any western dresses. She always wore sarees. Alisha maasi, on the other hand, was always well dressed in the latest fashion clothes.

'What is the plan for your birthday, Anuj?'

'I don't feel like celebrating my birthday.'

She sat next to me and ran her fingers through my hair. Her motherly love was hard to miss.

'I know why you don't want to celebrate. I would be really pleased to do anything to make your birthday special, son.'

'Auntie, I want to know more about my mom.'

'Sure. But what exactly do you wish to know?'

'Did Mom know about Soha?'

'You are still stuck there?'

I nodded, so she answered straightaway, 'Yes, she was aware of Soha.'

'Then why did she not say anything? How could she accept it?'

'Just because she did not discuss anything doesn't mean she accepted it, Anuj.'

'She never complained about Soha to me.'

'Maybe you were too young to understand such a thing. I am sure she wouldn't have wanted to burden you with such thoughts.'

'Maybe. But did she ever complain about Soha or Papa to you?'

'She was an obligation, Anuj.' She said with a straight face.

'Obligation? What do you mean?'

'I can tell you the truth, but would you be able to hear anything against your father?' she asked matter of factly.

'I guess I have seen enough in life.'

'Anuj, your father was always struggling for money. Your mother's medical expenses were all borne by that rich and cunning Soha.'

'Why did my father ask Soha for help and not you?'

'Your father and I were not on talking terms. You know, we don't get along too well.'

'But you loved your sister, and still did not talk to her? My mom hated Soha, and even then she tolerated everything?'

'It's not about me, dear. It's about your father,' she said resignedly.

Suddenly my Mom seemed like a mystery to me. I never knew my father was struggling with money. He had always made everything available to me, whenever I asked for it.

'Can I ask you something about Mom's letters?'

Alisha maasi fidgeted, as if I had asked something that made her feel uncomfortable.

'Which letters?'

'Her last letters. My mom had a habit of writing letters to everyone, I am sure you know that. During her last days, she had written letters for close relatives.'

'Yes, I know Anuj but...'

'There's something really weird, auntie,' I said, lost in deep thought.

'What?'

'She did not leave any letter for me,' I said, my voice cracking.

She was silent and her expression changed. I have learnt that anger is the most magnificent competition in which a human being can indulge. It brings out all that is best, and worst in us.

'I have no idea, Anuj. I have no idea why. But why don't you ask your father?'

15

Roshan

Soha earned a seat in MD in Gynaecology in the same medical college from where she was pursuing her MBBS. I, on the other hand, had stopped going to the shop as it gave me excruciating reminders of what I had lost. Although sometimes, when I couldn't resist myself, I would often pass by the clinic and get talking to Noor Clinic's guard, just to know what was happening in Soha's life.

Ironically, as much as I felt choked with everything that was happening to me, people around me were also feeling the same. The difference being that in their case, it was the increasing air quality index of the once-green and serene Delhi. Dust kicked up all day long as cars along Delhi's vast and growing road network contributed to the major share of pollution. They contributed to making Delhi one of the third most harmfully polluted cities in the world. I had no doubt that one day we would be topping the list. Environmental activists were protesting every day to ban diesel vehicles from Delhi. In a way, Delhi was a reflection of what I was feeling. I was drowning myself in my misery and helplessness.

If that wasn't enough, my meeting with Manisha was somehow taken as an affirmation by my parents to go ahead with the wedding. The wedding date was fixed within a week of our meeting. Needless to mention, my family was overjoyed. Even Dr Khan seemed to be cheerful about my wedding.

I wanted to talk to Soha. I guess I was not convinced yet.

I was in the shop since morning. My attention was unceasingly at the Noor Clinic. I had called the Clinic on their landline number three times already. The first time, I had enquired about Dr Khan, the second call had been about a fake appointment, and the third time, I had to disconnect the call quickly after hearing a male voice. After waiting desperately since morning, I finally saw my favourite face in the afternoon. She was dressed in a light green salwar suit and was heading towards the clinic. She entered the clinic before I could stop her. I walked up to the guard who was unnecessarily being rude with me, with every passing day.

I stood there facing the guard, looking at him in the eyes. I knew well that one stupid step from my side could escalate the tension with my father or Dr Khan.

'Hey, uncle.'

'Uncle ...?' The guard seemed to be a bit taken aback. Perhaps it was hard for him to accept such a sudden show of respect.

'Uncle, could you please inform everyone in the clinic that new stock of greeting cards has arrived at our shop.'

'Dr Khan needs greeting cards?' The guard probed.

'No, his daughter, I guess.'

He passed me a look that looked like my father's on seeing my school report card. I returned silently to my shop and wrote a one-line message on a greeting card.

*"Last meeting, 5 P.M.
Venue Pitampura garden"*

After one and a half hours, a striking voice fell into my ears.

'Uncle, where is the stock of the new greeting cards?' Soha asked.

My father was scratching his head, confused at which stock she was referring to. I called out immediately.

'Here is the stock.'

She walked towards the heap of the greeting cards I had pointed at.

I looked at her beautiful face and forgot everything. I wondered if she was the same girl who I had studied with and had dreamt my life with. I wanted to hug her, but knew that everyone's eyes were on us. I signalled her towards a small card in a red envelope. She picked it up, held that with a fake smile, and walked out of the shop.

Before I could get a hold of myself, my father asked, 'When did the new stock of greeting cards come?'

I flushed at not being able to give him an answer and pretended to be busy sorting some files.

At 5 in the evening, Soha and I were sitting below the same tree in the Pitampura garden. A smile was pasted on my face, just at the thought of her being there with me. The garden was dotted with many couples who would be dreaming of a future with each other. It was a comfortable place for us. The smile and the usual peaceful aura were missing in Soha, though. She was dressed in a pale pink salwar kameez and she had her dupatta wrapped around her head, partially covering her face. It led me to wonder whether she was hiding from others or me. Her small brown purse was half-opened form one side and the water bottle head was peeping from it.

She was continuously looking at the other couples and was checking her watch every five minutes.

I was so lost that I did not care for anything and asked, 'Can I hug you?'

She smiled and we hugged. I closed my eyes for a few seconds. Everything vanished and there was only the silence of eternity. She whispered into my ear, 'Why have you called me here, Roshan?'

We both parted and I replied, 'Actually, Papa is trying to fix my wedding.'

'Oh, with whom?'

'That is not important.'

'Then?'

'I want your decision. I would wait for you, Soha.'

'No dear, you should marry and move on. It's pointless to wait for me.'

'But why? Why can't we be together?'

'Because you are a Hindu and I am a Muslim.'

'So what?'

'Because Hindi starts from left, Urdu from the right; because you worship facing the east and we worship facing the west direction; we believe in the moon and you, the sun; and...' she sighed, 'You worship Ram, and we, Allah.'

'But we all have one god.'

'Where is god? Have you ever seen him?'

I shook my head.

'There are only religions and religious people; there is no god.'

'If there is no god, then what is the use of religion?'

She exhaled and looked at her wristwatch. Then she opened the small water bottle, took a sip and said, 'Roshan, I don't want to go against my family.'

There was silence. The hush whispered that Soha was trying hard to control her emotions.

'So you are okay that I will be marrying someone else?' I said after a long silence.

She looked at me and the tears in her eyes said it all.

'Is it your final decision?' I prodded.

'Will you come to meet me after the wedding?' Soha said changing the topic.

'Why? And what would be our relationship?' I almost yelled.

'We could be good friends.'

'Friends?' I flushed.

'In that case, we shall not meet.'

'But what if I want to meet you?' I was not in a proper frame of mind.

'We will not meet, but we would be there for each other when the need arises.'

'What if we both are in trouble?'

'Then we would marry.' We both laughed.

She stood and dusted her salwar kameez. It was a signal that the meeting was over. I followed her out of the park. She hired an auto and instructed the driver, 'Bhaiya, Rohini sector 16, DDA colony.'

We sat in the auto and even amid all the Delhi traffic, I was deaf. It seemed we were moving towards our destination in slow motion. She held my hand in hers. I looked at Soha and she was gaping at me in tears. I diverted my gaze and looked at the other end of the road.

'I promise I would never leave you when you are in trouble,' she said confidently.

The auto driver braked the vehicle, 'Madam, DDA flats are here. Where shall I drop you?'

'Take a left turn and halt near the Shani Mandir,' she replied.

Soha came closer to me and whispered in my ear, 'You are a good human being , Roshan. Now try to be a good husband.'

Before I could say anything, she kissed me and walked out of the auto.

⌘

As the date of my wedding drew closer, the house got more and more crowded with relatives, all excited and showering me with blessings. I must confess that even though initially I did not enjoy the teasing or excitement of my relatives a single bit, but eventually, I too got carried away with all the undivided attention that was being showered on me. I never thought I was so important to anyone. My father had a smile on his face for days because of me, and this was a rare sight. I couldn't help notice that from the usual Hitler face, his face had mellowed down to a serene, calm and joyous one.

A day before the wedding, a courier came for me; the sender was Miss Malini from Chandigarh. I picked the beautifully wrapped gift and read the card attached to the gift. The card had only two words "Best wishes" but the gift had words. It was a beautiful silver customized key chain with an engraving:

You are a winner and I am just a doctor.

⌘

Manisha was much loved and accepted by everyone in the family. She showed some great cooking skills, along with a loving attitude towards everyone. With time, I realized she was good at heart too. She was always there to help mom, and even my father had a different attitude towards Manisha. She got a lot of attention from my family. Although initially I felt jealous, but I was also really happy for her. She knew how to make someone feel special and had earned that special place in our house.

But my case remained the same. The wedding changed nothing for me. My Hitler father continued to look down upon me as if I was the most useless human on earth. Our book shop started getting a lot of competition from nearby sellers.

My legal practices still remained in a dying state and just as in the beginning of my career, clients stayed away from me. I started taking up basic works like creating rent agreements, notary, and property and wedding registrations, etc. Even if I didn't have a case in hand, I was starting to get some decent business from these basic jobs.

Before I could settle in my job or married life, Manisha got pregnant. Even though I was concerned about the future of our baby with no steady income in hand, I was ecstatic about becoming a father.

I desperately wanted to share the news with Soha. After the marriage, our contact had decreased to occasional courtesy messages during festivals. Oddly enough, my biggest worry about Soha was that one day, she would call and say that she had found someone special. In theory, I should have been happy at such a news. But the heart is a devil and it couldn't bear the thought of seeing Soha with another man.

After a few months, we were blessed with Anuj.

I was exhausted, terrified, overwhelmed and so very much in love with the littlest person I had ever seen. A part of me couldn't believe he was actually in my arms, while the other part of me felt like I had known him my entire life. For the first time ever, I could begin to understand how much my father loved me.

That evening, I typed the message thrice and deleted it, wondering how Soha would react to it. I did not know where I got the courage, but in the end, I messaged her, *I am blessed with a baby boy.*

Even before I could shake off the nervousness, her reply came, making me even more nervous: *Congratulations! Happy for you.*

I simply typed, *Thank you.*

She sent another message, which made me feel that Soha had taken the news well. *Was it a normal delivery or C section?*

Normal, I replied back.

I wish I would have been there to deliver the baby.

I did not send a reply. There was nothing I could have said to her.

With the new addition to the family, expenses had increased overnight. It was Anuj's first birthday and the entire family was expecting a big celebration. So I had to do something to avoid this huge expense. I decided to take a short trip to Haridwar with Manisha and Anuj on the pretext of getting blessings from god. My parents were joyous to hear that.

Taking a trip to Haridwar from Delhi was much more affordable and easy on the pocket in comparison to throwing a party for relatives and the entire neighbourhood. The public transport buses ensured the fare was affordable. The only thing left to arrange was the accommodation, which again was not an issue in Haridwar.

'I didn't know you were so religious,' Manisha said with a grin as we settled in the bus for Haridwar.

'Why? Because I am going to Haridwar?'

'No, because I know you do not believe in god. But still, thank you for doing this or else there would have been too many people for Anuj's birthday.' I felt bad when she said that.

'I came to avoid the expenses.' I rubbed my face and closed my eyes for a few seconds.

'I know, and you need not feel sorry,' she said while holding my hand.

'Alisha's wedding is round the corner, and we will have to gift her something. So it is better to save a bit right now.'

'You need not worry about that.'

'Thank you for understanding,' she said with a smile.

The air of intense spirituality in Haridwar absorbs one as soon as you enter. It has an enchanting aura about it that one can't miss. People who visit India make sure they visit Haridwar. The breathtaking city holds many religious festivals. I was busy taking in the view when Manisha probed, 'Can I ask you a question? It's a little personal.'

'Sure. Anything,' I encouraged her with a smile

'Do you often compare me with Soha?' My smile instantly flew out of the window. I went tight-lipped, but I also did not want to lie to her.

'It's okay, I got my answer.'

It pained me to see how Manisha's face struggled to fight the distress.

'Soha was an impractical dream for me, but you are my reality,' I said in a timid voice.

Suddenly the bus jerked, and it woke up Anuj. He started bawling. Manisha tried to pacify him and get him to be quiet, but he must have been startled badly. I took him from her and cradled him until he was sleeping peacefully again. There was something magical and peaceful about watching him sleep.

'I have a dream for Anuj,' she said. 'I want my son to be educated in the best school and have the best life possible.'

I nodded at her obvious love, and gently, she held my hand and said, 'I don't want my son to feel that he was born in a struggling family.'

Now I understood why she had said it was a dream.

'But then, how will we fund the expenses?'

'Hmm, don't worry. I have some jewellery; we will sell or pawn it to make sure that Anuj is sent to the best school in the city.'

'But why so much on education?' I asked wondering why Manisha was stressing so much on sending Anuj to best schools.

'My father couldn't send me to a good school and there were not many options for me to choose except for home science.'

I nodded.

'I want him to have his own idea of success.'

It just rubbed my own failure deeper. I looked at her as she said, 'I have one more request. Let us not add a surname to his name.'

'Why?' I asked shocked.

'He should not be known as a Hindu or a Muslim.'

16
Anuj

It was my eighteenth birthday, and since morning, I had been getting calls from my friends and relatives. Everyone seemed amused that I was turning eighteen, while I wondered what was the big deal! Except that I will finally be able to vote. The elections were close enough and Narendra Modi was fighting for the second term. I was getting calls from everybody, but I was waiting for one person to call.

Gagan called me around 10 a.m., which was unusually early for him, as he loved his sleep more than anything else, especially during holidays.

'Where are you Anuj?' Gagan shouted even before I could say hello.

'I am at auntie's house. What happened?'

'I am coming to meet you, be there!'

'You know today is my birthday, right?'

'*Kaminey*, why do you think I am calling you at 10 a.m.?'

'What does that mean?'

'Nothing!'

He disconnected the phone and for the first time since morning, I had a genuine smile on my face.

Alisha maasi had already asked me many times if I had any plans for my birthday. I politely denied any celebration.

I opened an old album that I had carried with me from home. There was a photo of the three of us, taken in Haridwar on my first birthday. My mother always loved to celebrate my birthday in Haridwar. I used to feel that my parents were too religious. I flipped through the album and landed on a beautiful image. I hugged the album and the photograph that showed my last birthday with mom. She had a huge smile on her face. On every birthday, she used to make greeting cards for me. In turn, I would try to copy her by making greeting cards for her on her birthday and anniversary. She was ecstatic every single time I gave her those averagely-designed cards. I closed my eyes and let myself be flooded with old memories.

Just then, I heard a knock at the door. It was one of the servants. 'Someone is here to see you, sir.'

'It must be Gagan... send him in, please.'

'I already invited him in, but he is refusing to come inside. He has requested you to come outside.'

I wondered why Gagan would say something like that. I concluded that it could not be Gagan. I went outside and saw who it was.

'Hello, Papa.'

'Happy birthday, Anuj.'

'Please come inside, Papa.'

'You know I will not. Alisha hates me.'

'But why?'

'Let's not talk about that today.'

I could see that he had something in his hands.

'I have something for you.'

'A gift?'

'It is a precious gift.'

'Papa, these formalities are not needed.'

I took the wrapped gift from him. It looked like some kind of a greeting card or letter.

'You need not open it here.' I nodded. 'This is not a gift from me. Your mom wanted me to give it you on your eighteenth birthday and she had arranged a series of letters for you.'

'This is from Mom?' I asked, taken suddenly by surprise. All this while I had wondered why she had not written to me. He nodded but I couldn't believe it. 'But how???'

'You can go inside and check.'

I nodded, too emotionally strung to say anything. My hands were shivering and my mind was blank.

'I think I should go,' he said softly.

I was so engrossed with the idea of my mother speaking to me for one last time through her letter, that for a moment, I couldn't register that my father was leaving.

I was too shocked to speak. It seemed he sensed my dilemma and explained, 'Your mother told me not to tell you about it until you turned eighteen.'

He turned to leave, but stopped. 'Can I have a hug from my son?'

We hugged each other and it gave me a strange sense of calmness. I felt we both needed this hug.

He whispered before leaving, 'I miss you, my son.'

I was still dazed and asked him, 'How were you hiding all these from me for so long?'

He smiled and said, 'Everything I never told you, my son.'

⌘

I rushed to my room and would have torn open the envelope if I wasn't scared of damaging the letter it held. I was too precious to be messed with. I opened it to see that there were two letters. On one letter, it was written, "Read me first". I hurriedly opened it.

Hello Anuj,
Happy birthday, my dear dear child.

How are you, my son? Have you been thinking what took this letter so long to reach you? I did not want you to read this until you turn eighteen, because I want you to be mature enough to understand life. Anuj, I have lived a happy life, but yes, there were a few challenges. When I got you in my life, I wanted all the best things for you. Unfortunately, destiny played a trick and deprived me of the only thing I wished with all my life – to see your success. But remember, son, irrespective of whether I am there physically or not, I will always be there with my family.

The best gift which I can give you is a better version of yourself. I believe that things happen for a reason, and they make us strong. I have asked your father to hand over a couple of letters that I have kept separately for you. I am going to take the liberty to ask you to do some things for me. I hope you won't mind doing it for me, son.

Each letter will have a task and instructions. Please don't question why I have decided such weird tasks for you. But I can promise you one thing - once you finish the tasks, you will be able to see a different Anuj in you. No matter who you are, no matter what you did, no matter where you've come from, you can always change.

You will only get the second task once you finish the first. Please don't share this with a lot of people. I am sure no one would understand the practicality of these tasks, but I also know that you would need someone to share this little secret with you.

Happy birthday once again, my son.

Miss you and your smile so much. Congratulations on becoming a full-grown man.
Love,
Mom

I had been feeling like I had been quarantined since morning, but suddenly, I didn't feel so lonely. I opened the other letter and read it quickly.

Go to a gurudwara and ask who got the flowers after Guru Nanak ji's death?
And remember, always choose the right question and the right person to answer it.

I read the first letter again and again. I took out the old greeting cards that Mom had given to me. This letter couldn't have been from Mom.

I almost screamed, 'It has to be Papa. This is Papa's handwriting. It is written by Papa!'

'No it isn't,' Gagan was standing behind me. I hadn't even realised when he came in and read the letter from behind me.

'When did you come?'

'Just a minute back.'

'Yaar, it's not written by Mom. Its Papa's handwriting.' I assumed he had read the letter.

'No, your mother has written that,' he said confidently.

'How can you be so sure?'

'Look at the bottom, yaar. It says "Love, Mom".'

I took a long breath. He was impossible!

'How long have you been standing here?'

Instead of answering me, he hugged me and shouted into my ears, 'Happy birthday, dude!'

'Thank you,' I said laughing at his antics.

'Who gave you these letters?' he asked me, eyeing the letters in my hand.

'I will tell you later.' He looked at me suspiciously. I had the sudden realisation that Gagan was a Sikh, and who else would be a better person to give me the answer to the question in the letter.

'Gagan, who got the flowers after Guru Nanak ji's death?'

'What?'

'Come on! You are a Sikh. You must know this!'

'How would I know, man?' He simply shrugged.

'Have you never thought about it?'

'I don't even know even how my grandmother died,' he said with a blank face.

Then the line from the letter struck me. Always ask the right question from the right person. Clearly, Gagan was not the right one.

17
Roshan

s days passed by, I fell deeper in love with Manisha than ever. She had managed to not only earn the love and respect of my family, but mine too. I had always thought I could never love again. During that time, Manisha's younger sister Alisha also got married. Her husband was from an influential family and was a leading BJP leader who worked in the South Delhi constituency.

Delhi was at its chaotic best during those times. Pollution was on the rise and so were the constructions for new flyovers and Delhi Metro. It all constituted to a big brawl. Growing air pollution and traffic were making our lives hell. But that was not the worst. Soon, Rohini was awarded with three new flyovers and our age-old shop and Noor Clinic landed right below one. For years, both the clinic and our shop stood proudly at the city's prime location. And now, everything had changed. Customer visibility and footfall had gone down tremendously. It was a setback for the entire area. Many a time we contemplated the idea of selling the shop, but no one was offering even half the price of what we were expecting.

Dr Khan's clinic was now managed by Soha. She had become a seasoned doctor. I often visited her clinic, especially whenever I needed to see a doctor. All these meeting were merely a patient and doctor meet and nothing beyond it. They were painfully courteous and professional. From Soha and Roshan, we had gone on to become Dr Soha and Mr Roshan for each other. However, one thing remained the same – she never charged anything from me. She was friendly with Anuj too. Initially, I thought Manisha had no problem with Soha, but once, when Gagan had a medical emergency and had gone to the Noor Clinic, Manisha shouted and screamed at Anuj for having suggested the place to Gagan.

It was an overreaction, to say the least. Anuj was just trying to help his best friend. Her behaviour might have confused Anuj, but to me, it spoke volumes. I secretly instructed Anuj never to visit Noor Clinic after that.

While the situation undoubtedly scared us all, we also did have some good memories. I remember it was an icy night in Delhi and Anuj had slept early. My father had gone to Lucknow to attend a wedding. Manisha, Anuj and I were the only ones in the house. We thought of spending some time together and sat down to watch television. The only thing being aired, at that hour, was some old movie that we had already seen many times over. So I decided to rent a movie so that we could enjoy the alone time we had received after months of hospital runs and worries.

I went out to a shop in our neighbourhood. 'Can I rent a VCR for a day?' I enquired.

'Yes, it's 300 rupees for the night.'

I made a face, but luckily, he gave me a good deal, which brought a smile on my face.

'Since you're also a shopkeeper, I will charge 200 rupees only.'

I might have refused such an amount in the name of entertainment, but it had been a long time since I had a moment of peace for myself. So I decided it was worth it. After an hour, he installed everything in the drawing room. Many wires were going from the TV to different boxes and it looked like a mini-theatre.

'Which movie are we watching?' she asked after seeing the elaborate setting that I had arranged. Happiness was evident on her face.

'It is a new Shah Rukh and Kajol movie.'

'I have already seen DDLJ three times, Roshan,' she said with a pout.

'It is not DDLJ. It is another movie – *Kuch Kuch Hota hai.*'

'The new one?' Her face brightened instantly.

I never thought Shah Rukh Khan could make my wife so joyful.

We settled on the sofa. The movie had two love triangles set years apart. The first half covered their friendship and life inside the college campus, while the second was the story of a widower's young daughter, who tries to reunite her dad with his old friend.

The movie ended at around 1 a.m. Manisha was wide awake and it was a surprise, since her medical condition always left her tired and exhausted.

'How was the movie?' I asked Manisha, who was resting with her head on my shoulders.

'It was such a nice movie.'

'Really? So what did you like best in the movie?' I asked, suddenly excited over how exultant and fresh Manisha looked. I had never realized how much she had weakened over the past few months.

'I liked the idea of the actress writing letters to her daughter.'

'Really?' I made a face. She had liked the letters more than Shah Rukh, Salman, Kajol or even Rani?

'What is so nice about writing a letter?'

'It's a nice thing, leaving something after you leave this world.'

I thought about her one-sided fantasies and said what would be the use of being remembered when you won't be there. You won't even see and feel it.

She held my hand and said, 'In the end, we are all just memories.'

⌘

It was Anuj's ninth birthday when Manisha fainted in the kitchen. Obviously, I panicked. Before I could call the doctor, she had regained consciousness. After that day, things kept getting worse for her. She started getting sick often and was always tired. We had gone to a couple of doctors, but nothing got better, neither her condition nor the doctor's promises. Soon enough, she was on one dozen tablets each day, just to be able to get through the day without fainting.

Manisha's condition had started affecting her badly. She initially had fatigue and upset stomach, but now she had developed disturbed cycles of menstruations as well. What bothered me was that she always hid how much she was suffering and it wasn't until I paid extra attention that I knew that her conditions were worsening with every passing day. Somewhere, I felt she never told me about her condition because she didn't want the extra medical expenses to weigh on me. I ignored all that and forced her to come with me to the doctor. After visiting multiple clinics, the problem remained unchanged. So finally I had to push her to visit Noor Clinic. Her hesitation was genuine, but seeing that I was adamant and was not going to take no for an answer, she finally agreed to consult Soha. I trusted Soha's diagnosis more than all the doctors we had met till now. I knew she would help me, no matter what. But there was a catch – that was the first formal meeting between Manisha and Soha.

Soha remained all professional, but there was awkwardness on Manisha's face. Soha conducted a few tests and asked us to visit again. But there was nothing in the diagnoses. She requested more tests in the next few visits and explained that she had to send the samples to some bigger lab. Two days later, Soha called me and asked me to come by her clinic the next day.

'Shall I come with Manisha?' I asked over the phone.

'No,' she replied sternly.

At her clinic, she spread a few sheets on the table and spoke for ten minutes, in between showing me various pictures and technical diagrams. She used millions of jargons and all the while, I sat there with a blank face

'Have you understood anything, Roshan?'

'Yes, Manisha is in trouble,' was all I could say.

She nodded and sighed. 'Let me make it simple for you. Your wife is suffering from ovarian cancer.'

Cancer should have been the thing that bothered me, but what bothered me was why Soha said, 'your wife'. She could have said Manisha.

⌘

My father was initially reluctant to have Manisha treated at the Noor Clinic, especially by Soha. But everyone knew about the financial liabilities associated with the disease. Ego works only when someone has money; else, everything is circumstantial. Sometimes I feel we all are hypocrites.

Manisha was diagnosed for epithelial tumours which grow in the cell linings of the surface of the ovary. It was the most common and dangerous kind that occurred in almost 85-90% women with ovarian cancer. Soha helped us to shift Manisha to Sir Ganga Ram hospital eventually.

Salpingo-oophorectomy surgery was done to remove the infected part, but the operation was not successful. I requested Manisha to get admitted at Noor Clinic. Although she was reluctant at first, she said yes, but on the condition that we would pay all the expenses. She did not want any financial obligations from Soha.

We knew Soha was the only person who would help me in any circumstances. Soha arranged a special room for us. After almost a year of treatments and visits, Soha's clinic had turned into a second home for me. Initially, I had shown my fake dignity and started paying the bills, but even though the pills had increased in number, the hospital bill remained the same. But one day, by mistake, the accounting department presented me with the right bill. I read it thrice, just to be sure. I understood that I was not paying even 20% of the bill.

I tried to ask for some money from distant cousins who were staying in Canada. They made some excuses about how they were struggling hard in another country. They promised to help the next year. I got a lot of sympathy and prayers from the entire world. While continuously sitting in the hospital, I realized that these blessings and sympathies were of no use.

The surgery, chemotherapy and tests. we had gone through with everything and there was nothing left to try and nothing left to fight. Alisha kept shuffling between the hospital and her home. She helped a lot by keeping Anuj with her. One fine day, she offered a *taveez* (amulet) and said, 'This will solve her problem.'

'Last time you gave her a ring with the same hope.' My frustration was evident in my voice.

Alisha looked at me and asked annoyed, 'Why are you staying in this hospital? Tell me!'

I looked at Alisha and decided to ignore her taunts. It was better to avoid nonsense than argue with no hope of a result.

I hate her show off and unnecessary exhibition of everything, but her presence gave Manisha confidence and me some space to gather my mind in solace. I walked out of the room, leaving the sisters alone in their world of comfort.

I returned almost an hour later and found Manisha by herself. 'When did Alisha leave?' I asked.

'A few minutes back,' she said. 'Could you please keep this in the bag?' She removed the taveez from her hand. I took it from her hand and when I opened the bag, I found that the bag was filled with many such religious souvenirs. I smiled.

'Why are you smiling like that?'

'See, how many people love you! It seems all the gods have sent special blessings for you through them.' I took out and displayed all the souvenirs on the bed.

'Remember this was given by Baba Akhandananad, and this taveez from Shirdi... and this one is from Salim Chishti...'

She smiled in pain, but remained silent.

I said, 'One life, one problem and so many babas.' She did not say anything.

Then suddenly, her expression changed and she laughed.

'What happened?'

'There are so many gods and millions of prayers and souvenirs, but no one to help me.' She sounded like she had already lost the battle. 'Roshan, I want a small favour from you.'

'Please tell me...'

'I want to write letters to everyone.'

I smiled and understood what she was trying to do.

I picked some pages and a pen from our stationery shop and gave it to her the next day. She was delighted to see it, but I noticed that after writing a line or two, her hands started shivering, making it impossible for her to write more.

'I know my handwriting is not good, but if you want, I can write them for you.'

She nodded.

She decided to write a letter to everyone – mausiji, Alisha, mamaji and even my Canada-settled cousins who never came or even asked how she was doing.

I wondered how she could be so forgiving and open-minded. I was thankful for these little letter writing sessions of ours; it had diverted our mind.

But all that apart, Alisha was still irate that her sister was getting treated at Soha's clinic. I know she doesn't like me too much, but still, I was relieved to see that she was there for her sister.

I still remember the day clearly. Manisha had lost a lot of weight and Anuj was sleeping on the attendant's bed.

'Manisha, you have written a letter to everyone. What about me and Anuj?' Alisha frowned.

'You did not write to us?' I said again.

She smiled, 'I have written something for you.' She signalled to a bag on the side table. 'Open that bag!'

How did she write the letter without my noticing her? Then I realised that Alisha might have helped.

I took the letter and looked at Manisha. 'Should I open it?'

She nodded. I opened the letter and noticed the broken handwriting. I could never imagine her beautiful handwriting to be so broken someday. She had tried hard to write, I knew, and there was one sentence only:

Never surrender, my hero.

I looked at her and for the first time, I realized how much I loved her. I held her hands softly in mine, went closer to her and summoned my courage to say, 'I love you. You are the best wife.'

18
Anuj

There was queer silence in the room. Both Gagan and I were lost in our solitary worlds. It seemed like my birthday had been forgotten completely. We went through every idea as to why, and most importantly, who had written the letter. We were trying to be Sherlock and Watson, but had now run out of ideas. When we couldn't come to a conclusion, our next step was to make sense of the contents of the letter. It was simply not making any sense at all.

'We should go to a gurudwara and ask someone?' Gagan said, after reading the letter loudly again, for the third time. 'Who got the flowers after Guru Nanak ji's death?'

'Is it about some garden?' Gagan looked at me.

I shook my head. 'How would I know?' I asked irritated with this never-ending discussion we were having since morning.

Gagan frowned. 'Why are you so worried about the flowers anyway?'

'Are you crazy or what, Gagan? I am not worried about the flowers. I am thinking who has written this letter.'

From the look on Gagan's face, I understood that finally, I had managed to make him understand what the real issue was. He looked at the letter and read it again and again.

'Was your mom watching *Kuch Kuch Hota hai* or *P.S. I love you?*' he asked casually.

'Gagan, please focus on the main point.'

'Hmm, why can't we ask your father directly?'

This was not going to work at all. I excused myself from the room and went to Alisha auntie. She was busy watching Shilpa Shetty's yoga classes on her 52" TV.

'Hey, birthday boy!' she greeted me in a cheerful voice.

'Auntie, I wanted to ask you something.'

'Sure. You seem cheerful all of a sudden. What happened?'

'Papa came, actually.'

Her expression mellowed down a little, but she asked politely, 'Why didn't you invite him inside?'

'I did, but he wasn't comfortable coming in,' I said hesitantly.

'Why would he?' She almost mocked at him. 'He will only go to Soha's house.'

'Auntie, today is my birthday...' Somehow I wasn't able to stand hearing anything against my father.

'Okay, sorry.' She shrugged.

'I have a request to make. I hope you will not deny. It is my birthday, after all.'

'What kind of request?'

'I just wanted to see the last letter that my mother wrote for you.'

'I have told you many times, Anuj, that is personal. Please don't ask for it again.'

'But what is in there that I cannot read?' Her expressions were not relenting, so I changed track. 'Fine! I only need a quick look. I just wanted to see Mom's handwriting.'

'You have so many greeting cards that were made by Manisha. Still, you wish to check her handwriting? Don't play smart with me. Tell me what happened!'

My face fell. I started to head back to the room, my heart sinking in gloom. 'By the way, that letter would not be of any use to you anyway, because your father had written it. Your mom was not well enough to write it herself. She dictated the letters and your father wrote them down for her... that's what I know.'

I smiled, as that solved the mystery. It was my father who had written that letter. But it was Mom's words, no doubt.

⌘

Gagan and I got into the Metro and headed towards Kashmiri Gate. We had to change to the yellow line Metro from there. It is always comfortable to travel in the Metro. No traffic, no pollution, and an air-conditioned ride. Through the entire journey, Gagan was silent and this was a little unusual for him. I was getting worried. I had never seen Gagan so silent. I looked at him, and to my surprise, he was staring at me.

'Why are you looking at me like that?' I asked a little taken aback and uneasy.

'Just wondering. Why would your mother write something like that?'

I sighed. The same thing had been bothering me as well.

'I know. I am also thinking the same.'

We finally got down at Patel Chowk. The famous Bangla Sahib Gurudwara was still approximately a couple of kilometres from the station. I had already been here many times with Gagan. He was not a religious person, but whenever his father pushed him, he pushed me as well to tag along.

Bangla Sahib is one of the most prominent gurdwaras in Delhi and is known for its association with the eighth Sikh Guru, Guru Har Krishan. I had a feeling that if we wanted answers, this would be the place. The Gurudwara had an aura that was unlike any other place. It always calmed me. I loved sitting by the sarovar, which was a huge pond that had many fishes.

We entered the gates and it was crowded. We left our shoes at the footwear deposit counter, took our token, and went forward. I covered my head with my handkerchief, as Gagan already wore a turban. Following the crowd, we proceeded towards the main hall.

Gagan went inside to offer his prayers, while I sat on the bank of the sarovar and started exploring the beautiful ambiance. The banks were filled with people. Some were taking a holy dip, while others enjoyed watching the fishes, just like me. The pond reflected the golden dome of the gurudwara and it was a sight to watch people and fishes, all moving around in its reflection. I looked around and my mother's task bewildered me a little.

Gagan came with prasad in his hand and sat beside me. I took one bite of the delicious halwa. This was my other favourite thing about coming to Bangla Sahib.

'So, any clues about the story of flowers?' I asked him.

'No, in fact when I was a kid, I had thought Guru Nanak ji never died.'

I looked at him with a dazed look.

'Actually, I thought he was god and it never made sense to me that he died.'

I merely nodded. 'So, whom should we ask then?'

'I have an idea,' Gagan said all of a sudden, giving me a little scare.

I looked at him and his excitement said that he had something dangerous in mind.

'Let's Google it.'

'No. It is not just a task for me. It is something given to me by my mother. So no short cuts.' Gagan shrugged.

'I wish Google was there when your mom was writing the letter. She could have found out easily.'

I made a face, wondering if Gagan made this all up or was he actually that silly sometimes.

'Can't we go to the place where Guru Nanak ji died?' I asked.

'Where Guru Nanak ji died? Do you even have an idea where that is? It is not in India,' Gagan was almost screaming into my ears.

'What are you talking about?' I asked Gagan and he quickly typed something into his phone. He showed it to me and I understood why he was behaving the way he did.

Guru Nanak ji's resting place was in Kartarpur, Punjab. The Punjab in Pakistan. My jaw almost hit the ground. What was running through my mother's mind?

'I know a person who sits on the first floor of the gurudwara. He is a guru here. I am sure he'd know the answer. He has even been to Pakistan.'

'Pakistan?'

'Sikhs visit Pakistan each year in thousands to celebrate the birth anniversary of their founder, Guru Nanak, at Nankana Sahib, his birthplace,' he told me.

'Ok, sounds nice....'

'But Guruji will be free only after the last prayer of the day.'

I nodded. I could wait.

The gurudwara fell a little silent around 9.30 p.m. and devotees started moving out. Gagan looked at me and that was the signal that we should move to the first floor.

It was neat and tidy, and many blankets and bed sheets were stacked in the corners. Every wall displayed the photos of Sikh

Gurus. We reached a hall and it was occupied. Close to about forty people were sitting inside, but there was pin drop silence. It seemed everybody was getting ready for a prayer session.

'Welcome Gagan,' one of the gurus came to us. With his slightly heavy built and a commanding body, he could easily scare his opponents. But the serene face and the gentle smile also put one at ease immediately. This was something that baffled me.

The way he called Gagan by his name and welcomed him, it seemed that they knew each other.

He touched the guru's feet and I too followed the same. He pointed towards a clean mat and we sat there thinking how to ask him our question.

Gagan asked, 'Guru ji, we just wanted to know the story of how Guru Nanak ji died.'

'Okay, but why all of a sudden?' We explained the situation and the problem at hand. He looked at me intently for a minute, as if searching my soul. He seemed impressed with the task Mom had set out for me.

And he smiled and began to narrate us the story.

Guru Nanak was the founder of Sikhism, and the first of the ten Sikh gurus. His parents, Mehta Kalu and Mata Tripat, were actually Hindus and had belonged to the merchant caste. Even as a boy, Nanak was fascinated by religion, and his desire to explore the mysteries of life. This eventually led him to leave his home.

It was said that when he was twenty-eight years old, he had gone down to the river to bathe and meditate and was gone for three days. When he reappeared, he was filled with the spirit of god and he said, 'There is no Hindu and no Muslim.' From thereon, he began his missionary work and the religion of Sikhism was born.

Guru Nanak's amazing spiritual personality, teachings, and love for humanity made him popular with both Hindu and Muslims.

Karatpur was the holy place where he stayed during his last days. Hindus, Sikhs and Muslims, all claimed him to be their prophet and were highly possessive about him. This eventually led to a dispute over the funeral rights. As the devotees became aware that the guru was preparing to leave his mortal coil, there was a stiff tension between Hindus, Sikhs and Muslims, all of whom claimed his body for the funeral rites. The Muslims wanted to bury the body as per their customs, while the Hindus and Sikhs felt it was appropriate to cremate his holy body. To put an end to the arguments, they approached the Guru to settle the dispute. Guru Nanak Dev ji talked to them in detail.

He explained to his devotees that his death shall be a unique kind of experience known as Joti Jot. This means, only his mortal body shall expire, but the light that is within his body shall be passed on to his successor. He asked his devotees to bring fresh flowers and asked the Hindus and Sikhs to place the flowers on his right side and the Muslims to place them on the left side. He instructed that the funeral rites shall follow depending on which set of flowers retained their freshness.

The day when Guru ji decided to leave his mortal body behind, he asked people to bring a sheet to cover his whole body and leave the place till the next morning. Devotees from all the three communities returned the following morning. When the sheet covering his body was removed, they were astonished to see that not a little trace of Guru Nanak Dev ji's physical body remained there. There were only fresh flowers, placed by all of them. All the flowers placed by all three communities remained fresher than before.

The Hindus, Sikhs and Muslims decided that they would build two separate memorials in praise of the Divine Master. Thus, on the banks of the River Ravi in Kartarpur, which is today a part of modern-day Pakistan, two shrines were built – one by the Hindus and Sikhs, and the other by the Muslims.

19
Roshan

I was fiddling with my phone and looked at my WhatsApp profile picture; it still had the image of me with Manisha. I had not changed that image for quite a while now. I tapped on the image and tried the change button, just to have a different image. I searched my gallery and picked an image of three smiling people – Manisha, Anuj and me. There was a smile on my face and it seemed like the picture was taken eons ago.

I closed my eyes and entered into the nostalgic sea of memories from the past, but there was a knock at the door, bringing me back. It was Soha. She was the only visitor to my house these days. Soha came inside the house, offering all the usual pleasantries. She went directly to the kitchen and pulled out the milk from the fridge. I was sitting silently in my own house. There was a time when we struggled to accommodate even a single relative, but now the house felt so vacant and huge.

'How was your meeting with Anuj?' she asked, mixing the coffee.

'Okay, I guess.'

'What happened? You look upset.'

'I am expecting Anuj today.'

'Why didn't you tell me before? I should leave early.'

'Relax!' I said with a smile.

After a while, she told me, 'I got confirmation about my research work.'

Soha was planning to research on 'Fertility and Surrogacy' from an institution in Europe. She had been trying to get admission for quite a while now.

'That is good news. How did you finally manage to get it?'

'You forgot, my brother is a permanent resident of Germany and works as a senior surgeon.'

'How long is the course duration?'

'Two years; it can stretch to three years as well.'

'Okay, and how is the clinic doing?'

'It's in a mess. It has been suffering ever since we got hit by that flyover. The complete area has turned into a dark zone. We only get a few underprivileged customers. There are new hospitals and health centres around now, that are providing all sorts of treatment along with allied services to serve all your medical needs under one roof.' She said it in one breath.

'Oh! So what are you planning to do?'

'I am thinking of selling off the clinic and joining some hospital after finishing my research.'

'Why sell the clinic? Don't you have any other option?'

'Other options are expensive and I don't have so much money saved. You know my condition. I am getting offers abroad. I may actually pick one and settle there.'

'What do you mean by settle?'

'Nothing Roshan.'

She might have ended the conversation at that, but many things were left unclear. I could see worry lines on her forehead. She desperately needed a family. I bid her goodbye as Anuj was about to come any time now.

I cleaned the room and placed all the things at the right place before tapping into the Zomato app on my phone. I had to order dinner. I looked at the entire menu and ordered Anuj's favourite veg biryani. I was contented that after a week, I would get to sit with my son and talk.

When Anuj came hours later, he was standing there with lots of question marks on his face. We exchanged a long, warm hug.

'How are you doing, Papa?'

'I am well. Come! Have you finished the first task in your mother's letter?' I asked him as he entered the house.

'Yes,' he said in a croaky voice. 'Can I ask you something?'

'Yes, but let's have dinner first.'

'No, that's okay. I don't want to put extra burden on you.'

'Burden?' He nodded and settled at the corner of the room. He was not comfortable in his own house. I went to the kitchen to arrange the food that I had ordered. Anuj remained seated in the living room, busy with his phone. He did not help me in the kitchen, which was otherwise our usual thing. Today, he was just sitting and digging into his smartphone, visibly uninterested in eating as well.

'Can you help in serving the food?'

He came to the kitchen and saw the food.

'Oh, biryani!'

'Yes,' I beamed.

We settled down on the table. Suddenly, his attention had diverted from his mobile phone to the food in his plate. Food has an amazing power; even the worst stuff begins to look good.

He took his first bite. 'Oh, you ordered from Behrouz Biryani?'

I nodded and before my happiness could go on, he asked. 'How did you know I was coming today?'

'You forgot that I too like biryani, Anuj.'

He went quiet and we had the food in silence.

I tried to break the silence and kept on asking about his friends, when he needed to submit the fee and whether he was comfortable in Alisha's house. It suddenly appeared that he had left the house long ago, when it had only been two weeks.

'Papa, can I ask you a personal question?'

'Seems like you have a lot of questions nowadays.'

'No Papa. Just one thing'

'Sure. Go ahead!'

'Why don't I have a surname? Why was I not named Anuj Dixit?'

'That is something personal.'

'Is it because it is related to Soha?'

'No, Anuj! It's related to your mom.'

I finished the last bite of the biryani and picked both the plates, moving towards the kitchen. He cleaned his hands and kept standing there, as if demanding something he deserved to know. He looked at me and said, 'I am getting late.'

'If you can avoid the luxury of Alisha auntie's place for a bit, you can stay here.'

'No Papa, some renovation is happening at her house. She had asked my help this morning. It would be really great if you could share the next letter from Mom.'

'Renovation? This is the third time she is renovating her home in the last three years. Crazy lady!'

'Papa....'

'I know you are here just for the letter.'

I was waiting for him to say he had come to meet me, if only to make me happy. But he did not. I went to my bedroom and he followed me. I pulled the letter from below the wad of clothes in my cupboard. He was fidgeting consciously. His excitement was evident.

I gave him the second letter and he opened and read in disbelief.

'Do you know what she has written in the letter?'

'Obviously. I wrote them...' I took a pause '...on your mother's request.'

'This is too weird. Why would Mom do this?'

'Nothing is weird. She loved you the most. She had written many letters and you know she loved writing letters.'

He gazed the letter again.

'Try to read between the lines,' I told him.

Hi Anuj,

Here is the next task for you, my son.

Go to Jama Masjid in Ramadan. Don't purchase, but ask for food from around the masjid.

Ask someone about shahada and also why there is no god other than Allah.

With love,
Mom

Note: Always ask the right question from the right person.

20
Anuj

Why would my mother force me to go to some masjid? How did my father know that I was coming home? He had ordered a meal for two. Or did I just eat Soha's share of dinner? But Soha doesn't eat Biryani. She hates spicy food, even my father. Only I love the biryani.

I came out of the house with a web of queries hammering my head.

I checked on Google and realised that Ramazan period was going on. I smiled at my mom's plan. Gagan and I decided to go to Jama Masjid. We got down at Chawri Bazaar Metro station and headed towards our destination in a rickshaw.

Jama Masjid was only one kilometre from the Metro station. It was my first visit to Jama Masjid, or any masjid for that matter. It sits across the road from the Red Fort at the end of Chandni Chowk. It was the modern-day leftover of a once-grand but also chaotic thoroughfare of crumbling yet characterful Old Delhi.

Gagan and I stood outside the gate. I read aloud the instructions written on the wall at the entrance. All Indian visitors must pay fifty rupees while foreigners had to pay three hundred rupees for entry to the Masjid. We paid the money on the counter and got tickets for ourselves.

'Now Gagan, this is a Muslim area, so let me talk to them and you are not going to say anything.'

He nodded. I started walking towards the gate and suddenly he looked scared. I frowned.

'What are you so scared about?'

'Because I am a Sardar, and people would notice the difference.'

'So what? I am also a Hindu.'

But Gagan seemed to be frozen and too afraid to take a step into the Masjid premises. So I decided to let him wait for me outside, while I went inside the Masjid. Suddenly an auto stopped in front of us and a young and beautiful girl stepped out of the auto. She passed a look at Gagan while adjusting her hijab and then headed towards the Masjid.

I was still wondering how to move towards the Masjid when I saw Gagan walking rapidly, almost past me. I wondered what had finally persuaded Mr Gagan to move his ass. I followed him and shouted, 'Wait for me, Gagan.'

'What happened? Why the sudden change of heart?' I asked as soon as I caught up with him, but Gagan was still almost sprinting in his steps.

'Where is that girl?' he asked, looking around frantically.

I fumed. So this was what made him walk so fast when nothing I said to him worked.

'Mr Gagan, we are inside the Masjid, so let us behave properly or else...' That was when Gagan and I actually had a look around. It was a Friday afternoon and Jama Masjid was flooded with people.

'Fuck, there are so many people here,' I exclaimed. Even before I realised, I had just cussed loudly in a religious place.

'Control, we are in a Masjid!' Gagan reminded me this time, and that too with a big grin of having caught me doing something bad.

There was a strange silence even with a sea of people inside. We sat at the corner and wondered what to do next. I opened Mom's second letter.

I wondered who would be the right person to ask this. I looked at all the faces which were either busy or lost in spirituality. Before I could plan anything, Gagan declared a national calamity. 'I am hungry.'

'Gagan, I am not allowed to buy and eat anything. We have to borrow something to eat.'

I understood that it was pointless to just sit there and wait. I tried to divert his attention towards the beauty of the mosque, but after every minute, he pleaded for food. The third namaaz of the day was about to begin. We decided to leave the place before that.

We went outside and I understood that it was not just Gagan who was hungry. In fact, we both were starving.

'Gagan, you go ahead and eat something.'

'Are you not coming with me?' he asked at how I had chosen to stay back. I was about to say no, but my stomach was roaring loud.

'Okay.' I nodded.

We both started searching for food corners.

We came out of the gate. Just then, the loudspeaker came to life, echoing the prayer. We walked on the lanes around the Masjid and Gagan's eyes were busy searching for lip-smacking non-vegetarian food. Karim's, opposite Gate no. 1, is an iconic Delhi restaurant. It's been in business since 1913. There was also another renowned restaurant next to Karim's, Al Jawahar. We crossed to the lanes where both the shops were situated, but as we reached there, we found out that both the shops were closed.

In fact, all of the popular food joints were closed.

'What the hell? Every joint is closed,' Gagan blurted his frustration.

His temptation of eating a good non-vegetarian dish had turned into a search for food for survival.

While we were searching for other food joints, I noticed an old man wearing a white cap and loose white clothes, staring at us. It seemed, he had just finished his namaaz. The way he was staring seemed like he could recognise Gagan. The man suddenly walked towards us and stopped right in front of Gagan

'Aren't you Gagandeep Singh?' Gagan nodded.

I was right. The man must have known Gagan from somewhere.

'You know him, how?' I asked the man out of curiosity.

'Yes.' The man nodded and continued. 'He often comes to my shop.'

'That's right,' Gagan said with a huge smile.

'Are you hungry?' the Muslim man asked.

I looked at Gagan and understood that our hunger was visible on our faces. Before I could reply anything, Gagan nodded.

'Come to my shop. It is Ramadan. Everyone is observing fast, so the shops will only open after 7 p.m.'

I looked at the buildings around. All of these people were observing the Ramadan fast. They will be fasting the entire day, but still they all seemed content.

After a few steps, we reached the shop, but like every other shop around, this one was closed too.

'But it is closed,' I said in surprise.

'It's closed from outside. You can get some food behind the curtain. Let me check what I can arrange for you,' the man said and went inside.

'How do you know him?' I asked Gagan as soon as we were alone outside.

'I have been here in the past. This shop is in the proximity to Gurdwara Sheesh Ganj Sahib. I often visit that gurudwara,' Gagan replied.

I had a strange feeling about the place and the restaurant. The man appeared to be a bit ill-mannered too. He did not even ask us what we would like to eat. We had been there for fifteen minutes and he hadn't even shared the menu yet.

After a while, he came out with one plate of food in his hands. He invited Gagan to the dining area. The restaurant was empty. It was not a fancy place, but just the number of plates and the size of the tandoor said that it was a popular eating spot and had a regular flow of customers.

The walls were decorated with quotes. And then, suddenly my eyes landed on one quote.

There is only one lord.

And another poster which said, *There is no god except Allah.*

He placed the sandwiches on the table and before I could say that this was not what we wanted, he served them to Gagan, who started hogging.

I looked at him getting satiated with each bite. The growing sounds from my stomach challenging me hard, I started losing my control. But before that, I couldn't resist myself from asking.

'Chacha jaan, you have nothing for me?'

'Oh, you are not keeping the Roza?' he asked.

I shook my head, but Gagan was unaltered.

'No, but why did you not ask this question from him?' I asked pointing towards Gagan who was still busy eating.

'Because he is a Sardar and I thought you were a Muslim.'

'Actually, I am a Hindu.'

'Oh! I am sorry.'

He went inside and returned after a few minutes with one more plate of sandwiches. Gagan had already finished his plate and looked content, as if a great storm had passed away.

I was looking at the walls around me. One wall had the image of Mecca. All the walls were painted in green. The religious affinity seemed to be in full display. Gagan, having a full stomach now, was busy replying to his girlfriends on Instagram. I started eating in silence. The man sat just next to our seat, but his gaze was in Jama Masjid's direction.

'How was the sandwich?' he asked after I was done eating.

'It was good, thank you,' Gagan answered for both of us.

He was cautiously looking away from us while enquiring about our wellbeing. He asked about my place and everything else to the point of being intrusive, but never once looking at our direction, which I found weird.

'We should get going,' Gagan said.

The man came to collect the plates.

'You want tea or coffee?' he asked while cleaning up after us.

I shook my head indicating a 'no' to his offer.

Now he came and sat facing us.

'Sorry, I was fasting since morning and I did not want to be tempted by food. That is why I was looking in the opposite direction when you were eating and we were talking.'

I looked at Gagan. There was guilt on his face. I felt ashamed about being quick to judge.

'How much is the bill?' I asked.

He smiled. 'How can you ask the bill in Ramzan?

'But we are not Muslims.'

'At the end of the day, you also belong to Allah,' he said with a calm face.

His words were unrealistic and illogical and suddenly Gagan asked, 'Why is there only one god, and no other than Allah?'

Many volcanoes ignited inside me. I was standing outside the Jama Masjid and questioning Allah. I was scared of the consequences. Gagan looked at me and shrugged.

'Please have a seat.' The man pointed to the seats that we had just emptied. We both took it silently, fearing the man's wrath.

'You know Islam originated in Arab, right?'

We nodded. He started telling us in detail.

The Arab area was largely dry and volcanic, making agriculture difficult, except near the oasis or springs. The landscape was dotted with towns and cities, two of the most prominent being Mecca and Medina. Medina was a large flourishing agricultural settlement, while Mecca was an important financial centre for many surrounding tribes. Communal life was essential for survival in desert conditions.

In pre-Islamic Arabia, gods or goddesses were viewed as protectors of individual tribes, their spirits being associated with sacred trees, stones, springs and wells. Along with being the site of an annual pilgrimage, the Kaaba shrine in Mecca housed 360 idols of tribal patron deities.

To unite them all, they started saying there is only one god, Allah. Allah is omnipresent and powerful. We don't know how he looks and who he is, but that he loves us and we are meaningless without him.

I found it a bit difficult to absorb and looked at Gagan. We both seemed confused and in disagreement.

'What is shahadah?' Gagan asked.

'It means declaring belief in the oneness of god.' He looked at Gagan.

'Sikhs and Muslims believe in a formless god. Both religions don't propagate against idol worship,' he said to Gagan.

'I agree.' For a moment, it appeared like Gagan would change his religion.

'So, who is Allah?' I asked confused.

'Allah is the same who Christians and Sikhs call as god, and Hindus know as bhagwan. We, Muslims, call him Allah.'

'So all religions are the same?' I couldn't get my head around it.

'No, all religions are fundamentally different, but superficially the same,' he said with a smile.

I rubbed my chin and asked,

'If all the religions are the same, then why are Muslims not allowed to marry outside their religion?'

'My dear, you are mixing god and religious practices. There can be a different prophet and different practices, but there is only one Allah.'

I was getting more and more confused.

'If there is only one god, then why do we, I mean Hindus, have so many gods?'

'Frankly speaking, it confuses me too. When all the other religions talk about one god, how do Hindus have so many gods?'

Before I could say anything, Gagan asked, 'So you mean all Sikhs and Muslims are the same?'

He smiled and said, 'If god is the same, then we all are the same too.'

21

Roshan

'Unsafe', 'rude', 'show off', 'last place I would want to go' – these were the new labels that were given to Delhi by the media. My Delhi had changed and was very different. It had taken on the tag of being the most polluted city in the entire world. But to those who had called the city home for years, there was no place quite like it.

The city was dominated by huge flyovers and long metro tracks. Aam Aadmi Party ruled the state. Our stationery shop had closed long back and now a pharmacy shop was in its place. Though I was still the owner, I had rented it out to the pharmacy. It was also the major source of earning for me. I often helped out Soha in her clinic, whenever time permitted. And because of the whole flyover thing, even Noor Clinic was struggling to get customers.

But amidst all this, I had other things that troubled me a lot more.

Anuj had finished his second task and I was sure that his doubts towards the letters would have increased manifold. But I was gleeful in the thought that Anuj would be coming home today. As a result, there was a child-like excitement in me. I informed Soha not to come that day. I cleaned and organized the house.

I checked my reminder file, where I still collected the printed copies of all the bills. I wanted to be up to date and had many fat files. Anuj always laughed and called me old school. He even tried to teach me how to do all that on my phone or laptop, but I would pretend to not understand anything. A smile came onto my face on its own, thinking about him.

I opened a file. It had all the details about Anuj's college admission. It had the receipt of payment of one lakh rupees against the first instalment of his fee. His seat was confirmed, but before the college opened, I had to arrange for another two lakhs.

I opened another file which carried the details of the rent I received from the pharmacy. That got me worried. I closed my eyes and thought about Manisha, about how we had committed to giving the best education to our son. The walk down the memory lane was halted by the knock at the door. I only had two visitors these days and I had already asked one to not come.

'Welcome, Anuj,' I said as I opened the door.

There was a genuine smile on his face this time and it cheered me up a bit more. We hugged and I closed my eyes, trying to forget everything for a few seconds.

'How are you, Papa?'

'Same as before,' I said with a smile.

He got settled like a guest on the sofa. He looked at the photo of us in the drawing room thrice. There was a smile on his face, on seeing his mother's picture. I had made dal and rice for both of us.

'Food is ready. I will just serve,' I told him.

'Oh Papa, I am not too hungry yet.'

'It's not about you, my boy. I am starving,' I said light-heartedly.

'Then why did you cook for me too?'

'Nothing like that. I usually cook only once, so I can eat the same thing in the evening too.'

'So if I eat this, then you will have to make something for dinner again?'

I smiled on hearing this and served the dal-chawal with some pickle, papad and a rich salad. Just the way we liked it. He took a spoon and had his first bite; I could look at him all day, watching him savouring the food. It is always so satisfying to see your kids eating.

'Why is there so much dust in the house? Isn't the maid coming these days?'

'No, Alka is not coming nowadays.'

'What happened to her?' he asked.

'I let her go, as there was nothing much to do in the house.'

He simply nodded to my comment. I hoped he wasn't thinking anything else.

'Have you finished your mom's second task?'

He nodded again in response.

'How is the food?' I asked trying to keep up the conversation.

'Oh, dal is awesome and you know I love rice.' He passed a contented smile.

'So, what did you learn? You must have been to the Masjid as a part of the task,' I wanted to be subtle.

'Yes, I went there and noticed that no one would go hungry from the Masjid during Ramzan.'

'Just that?' I took my chance.

'Yes, and that food has no religion,' he said without emotion.

'How is your Alisha maasi?'

'She is good.' Then he abruptly changed the topic, his voice laced with concern. 'What is the deadline to submit the next fee instalment? Did you get any follow-up email from the college?'

'Yes, everything is good and will be taken care of before the session begins.' I sighed and faked a smile, trying hard to hide the worry on my face.

We had finished with our meal and were clearing up the table. 'Papa, I must leave.'

'Why can't you stay here? What is so special at your maasi's place?' I said in exasperation.

'Nothing! It's just that I'm not comfortable here.'

'I know Alisha's home is fully air-conditioned and has all the modern facilities unlike ours...but...'

'You know the truth, Papa.' He heaved a sigh. 'You know that is not true.'

I did not want to take this discussion any further. 'Here is some pocket money for you.' I took some cash out of my pocket and handed it to him.

'No, Papa, I don't need more money. I have enough with me.'

'I know. Just keep this, in case you need it sometime,' I insisted.

'Thanks, Papa.'

I could sense that he was a little hesitant. His eyes were looking for something, for which he had come here, but I was waiting for him to ask for it. After a few minutes of silence, he finally spoke.

'So, where is the next one?'

'Are you looking for something?'

'My mom's next letter.'

I handed the piece of paper without any emotion. This time, there was lesser enthusiasm in him for holding his mother's letter. He just took it from my hand and placed it inside his pocket. I was surprised at why he did not even bother to open it.

He was all set to leave for the day and then he asked the brewing question, which he had been hiding for a long time. 'Papa, I wanted to ask you an awkward question. Hope you will not mind...'

'Is it related to Soha?' I asked.

'Yes.'

'Go ahead.'

'Assuming the events that would have happened in the past, I want to know what Soha's father said to you, when you asked about her?'

'Why does that matter to you, Anuj?'

'I just need to know, Papa. Please...'

'He said he would accept me if I convert to Islam.'

22

Anuj

I went to meet my father and returned with my pocket warm with extra cash. I realized how much we take things for granted and assume that certain tasks were an obvious duty of the other person, without even thinking of sharing the load. I had noticed many things and it bothered me a bit.

Why had he fired the maid for no reason? Was it because he was unable to afford her? Why was he cooking himself now, when he had been perfectly okay with ordering?

I did not open the letter. I messaged Gagan to come to auntie's house if he was free. By the time I reached auntie's house, Gagan was already there, waiting for me. I looked at him and I felt so lucky to have a friend like him, who would drop everything and come to me in the blink of an eye.

'So, what is the next task?' he asked as soon as he saw me. So he knew that I must have got the next letter, which like the previous ones, would carry another task.

'Let's go inside and talk,' I directed him towards my room.

I saw that auntie was busy on her phone, probably chatting with the entire world. Sometimes I felt she was too social and had given up her personal space completely.

The house was filled with labourers who were busy renovating. It seemed that the house was up for a change completely. Almost half a dozen people were working just with the colours of the wall. This time, it seemed that the walls were taking on a more artistic turn than the traditional solid walls. Even though it was only half done, the paint job was coming out really impressive, with its fancy texture and artwork.

One the other hand, there were a couple of workers who were scrubbing and polishing every piece of furniture in the house, to make it shine like brand new.

I observed all this silently for a while and then eventually went back inside the room with Gagan.

'You don't seem too excited about the letter. What does it say this time?' Gagan asked as soon as he settled on the bed in my room.

'I don't know. I have not even opened the letter yet.'

'You have not opened your mom's letter yet?' Gagan asked, amazed.

I pulled out the white envelope from the bag and gave it to him. He looked suspicious and frowned.

'This is the third letter from my mom. Go ahead and open the envelope.' I handed Gagan the envelope, who still seemed to be reluctant to take it from me

'Why do you want me to open the letter? Shouldn't you be opening it?'

'Because I want to guess the task without reading it.'

'What?' Gagan was clearly getting more and more confused.

'Just open it!' I said forcing the letter into his hands.

He still didn't seem to be sure about opening it, but my stern expression conveyed everything. So he carefully opened the letter and read it.

'Let me guess,' I said before he could read the letter out loud. 'So the next task is related to a church, probably comparing it with different religions?'

Gagan smiled on my blind guess and handed the letter to me.

Hey Son!
This time, you need to go to a church.

Find out what is the difference between Jesus, Muhammad, Guru Nanak and god?

PS: Always ask the right question from the right person.

Love,
Mom

'How did you guess that?' Gagan asked watching me grin mischievously, but I didn't answer his question.

'Where should we go, Gagan? I want to get this task done quickly.'

'I think we should go to some church this Sunday. That would be the best time,' he said intelligently.

'That's great. We will go to church on Sunday.'

After Gagan left, my brain kept working over and over again on the tasks and what they meant. A series of red flags popped in my head. First the gurudwara, second a masjid and now a church. Everything seemed clear to me.

I looked at the calendar. Sunday was still five days away. I looked at the question again and thought to search for the answer on Google, but my conscience told me it would be cheating. Even though my brain screamed that this was my father playing tricks with me, I still didn't want to disrespect something that was in my mother's name. So I decided that I will go and seek the answers from the relevant person rather than taking a short cut. But the truth was, that in spite of saying yes to the plan with Gagan, I was in no mood to visit any church. Just then, I remembered that my history teacher from a couple of years back had been Christian. He would definitely know the answer.

I scrolled through my contacts, searching for his number.

'Hello, George sir? This is Anuj. I met you at the school function a few days back?'

'Oh yes. Hi, Anuj! What a pleasant surprise. How are you?'

'Good sir, I wish to meet you. Can you suggest a good time to meet?'

'Sure. But what is this regarding?'

'I had a few questions related to history and religion.'

'Okay, can you meet me today?'

'That'll be great! Should I come to the school then?'

'No, I am actually at the church for some personal work.'

I went quiet. Here I was, trying hard not to go to church. He broke my thoughts and asked, 'Anuj? Can you come to church?'

23
Anuj

For me, Christians were those who prayed only on Sundays at the church, and maintained a western lifestyle. Drinking was not a taboo in Christianity and even their god drinks. Ignorance has its own assumptions.

I changed into a plain white shirt because I had always seen well-dressed people in the church and I didn't want to look out of place. It took me around twenty minutes to get dressed and when I looked into the mirror, I realised at best, I looked like a rich waiter. I removed my blazer and sat exhausted on the bed, wondering why I was being made to do all these strange things. I sat there for a few minutes and decided that my normal T-shirt and jeans were going to be enough.

'Where are you going?' Maasi called out.

'I am just going out to meet my teacher.'

'At the school?' she asked curiously.

'Church!' I said in hesitation.

Her eyes held so many questions as she said, 'First, you went to a gurudwara, then a mosque, and now you're going to a church?'

I looked at her. With her mobile phone in one hand and the other hand resting on her hips, she looked like a detective interrogating a suspect. Watching me being silent and not giving an answer, she sat on the sofa and sighed loudly.

'There is nothing wrong with going to a church, mosque or anywhere, but why all of this so suddenly?'

'Because my mother...' I could not complete the sentence.

'Your mother? Anuj, what is this stupidity you have got yourself into?'

I knew that whatever I would say to her would only give her more ammunition for my father.

'It's something personal, auntie,' I blurted.

⌘

A famous church, attracting hundreds of tourists and locals alike, Sacred Heart Cathedral in Ashok Place was built completely of red bricks, in Eastern European architecture style. George sir had asked me to meet him there by noon. After reaching the church, I called George sir and he asked me to come inside. I removed my shoes and socks, but noticed that there were no others shoes anywhere. I kept my shoes unattended at one side and moved inside the church.

The church was designed to accommodate roughly three hundred people. It was a fine example of the architecture of colonial India. The glass and marble work of the Cathedral was perfectly preserved even after more than fifty years of its establishment.

Inside the church, in the main hall, I found a small gathering of people who were practising some songs. With a little struggle, I finally managed to find George sir in the crowd. With his big fat belly and dark moustache, it was not so tough to spot him. He had hair in abundance, almost all over his body, except on his head. He walked like an old, bald wrestler. I was pretty certain that he could win a war against humanity, single-handedly.

'Good afternoon, sir,' I greeted him politely.

'Where are your shoes?' he asked, noticing my bare feet.

'I left them outside, sir.' It was then that I noticed that everyone was wearing their shoes.

'In here, you can wear your shoes. Please be comfortable and wear your shoes, and meet me there.' He pointed me to a corner seat. I went outside, grabbed my shoes, went to the washroom and cleaned myself. Everywhere I looked, there were women and girls in normal clothes instead of formal skirts that I had assumed. I concluded that all those movies that I had watched were made in Hollywood, and hence, it was not true for Indians probably. Everything seemed so perfect in movies. Reality, on the other hand, was so different and almost so average.

I went into the corner. He was sitting with his eyes closed. It looked like he was praying. I remained silent and looked at other people, and noticed that everyone was reading something. There were so many books and silence prevailed in the room. Then I heard snoring. I looked around and there was no one within twenty-five metres.

I failed to find the source of the sound and then I heard it again. When I looked at George sir, he was silent, but his body was moving with every breath. He wasn't praying; he was sleeping.

'Sir!' I nudged him gently to wake him.

He was unmoved. I poked again and after the fourth call with a little stronger poke and nudge, I managed to wake him.

He opened his eyes with a sudden jolt and then realised he had fallen asleep on the seat.

'Oh, I am so sorry. So, you said you had a question for me?' Sir said while he rubbed off sleep from his eyes and sat upright.

'Yes sir!'

'Related to history?'

'No. Related to religion.'

'Okay....' He seemed to be a little puzzled.

'Was Jesus a god?' I asked without waiting and wanting to get this over with as quickly as possible.

'What? What kind of a question is that, Anuj?'

I was silent. I hoped that he would answer without all the background to the question.

'Jesus was not god. He was the son of god,' sir said, saving me from explaining anything.

'Then who is his mother?'

'Mother Mary.'

'So is god a male or female?'

'God has no gender,' he said, slightly hesitantly this time. I am sure he was wondering what I wanted. He stared at me as if I was announcing the third World War and he had to fight against Germany.

'In Christianity, God is addressed as the Father. Partly because of his active interest in human affairs, partly because like a father, he takes care of his children who are dependent on him. Just like a father, god too responds to humanity as his children, acting in their best interests. But why are you asking such questions, Anuj?'

'I'm confused about god.'

'What is the confusion?'

'How many gods do Christians believe in?'

'One.'

'That is my confusion exactly. Christians, Sikhs and Muslims, all say that there is only one god. So are they referring to the same one?'

'In Christian belief, the name of god has always had much deeper meaning and significance than being just a label or designator. It is not a human invention, but has a divine origin and is based on divine revelation.'

I realized he was a complex man and I should ask the most relevant question.

'What is the difference between Jesus, Muhammad, Guru Nanak and god?'

'Oh, that is a complex question. There is one god and Jesus, Mohammad and Guru Nanak are all the messengers or prophets of this god.'

'What are the chances all these beliefs are mentioning the same god?'

'What makes you think so?'

'No one has seen god, and all these religions say there is only one god. Means they worship the same god?'

'Yes, maybe... Hmmm.... Not sure.'

'Why are we separated into different religions?'

'Religion was made by humans. So you can have as many as you want... but god is one,' sir simplified.

I was silent and he took my silence differently.

'Are you confused about which one is the best or which one you should follow?'

'No, I was wondering, if there is only one god, then why all the hassle and discussion over which is better?'

I shook my head as he continued, 'Check all the scriptures, *Guru Granth Sahib*, *Bible* and *Quran*, they are all different in their forms, but take on the common thing. Because it says majorly one thing in common, at least that has to be true.'

'What is that?'

'I already told you, that there is only one god.' Sir finally smiled. But looking at my face, he asked, 'Are you still confused?'

'Yes,' I sighed. 'Why do Hindus have so many gods?

'No clue,' he said politely.

⌘

I had finally understood what my father had wanted to convey. Somewhere in my heart, my respect for him had grown. I was resting on my bed and wondering how things were moving ahead. My friends were posting images with their girlfriends and their vacation spots. Some, who were still struggling to get admission in colleges, had turned into Karl Marx and were posting inspirational quotes, questioning humanity.

I, on the other hand, had landed myself in a completely different world. People my age didn't embark on a journey to search the meaning of human existence, god and religion. This all had started with my father wanting to marry a Muslim woman. Now it was the matter of which was the best religion. It seemed like I was living in some kind of a mythological world.

'How was your visit to the church?' Maasi asked while calling me for dinner.

'I did not go to the church. I went to school instead,' I lied to her.

'Okay, come for dinner! Food is ready.' I nodded and joined her on the dinner table. As usual, they were chatting together.

'What happened, Anuj? Why are you so quiet today?' Uncle asked almost suddenly between his bites.

'Oh nothing, uncle.'

'Your father had called up today. He was asking where you were, because he could not reach you. From his voice, it seemed he was not feeling well,' uncle said.

'Nothing to worry, then. He is in the best hands, with a free doctor to take care of him,' auntie said, interrupting uncle.

Suddenly I found it tough to eat. I looked at them, but I did not wish to appear weak in front of them. In the meantime, uncle finished his dinner and moved out with an excuse to call someone urgently. Auntie and I were left at the table, staring at each other. I understood that she was not going to leave me easily and her eyes were continuously demanding an answer. Before she could voice her trail of queries, I shot mine.

'Why do you hate other religions?'

'I knew it! This is about that ridiculous Soha, isn't it?'

'No, it is not, auntie. I didn't even ask about her.'

She understood that I had not liked her comment, 'Sorry for being rude.' I waved it away with my hand, gesturing it was okay.

I repeated my question. 'Why do you hate Muslims?'

'I don't hate Muslims, Anuj. I hate Soha.'

This was new. Suddenly it appeared that everyone around me was secular, and I wondered why I had so much hatred in me.

'Sorry to ask again, but why do you hate Soha so much?'

She sighed loudly and her expression changed completely. 'She was waiting for my sister to die, so that she could marry your father. That is why she never got married. She has always been a money-minded lady.'

'Money-minded? What are you talking about? She has always helped our family.'

She came and sat near me. 'Why do you think she is so soft on you? Don't you ever wonder why a well-educated and rich doctor like her is interested in your father, who barely earns anything?'

'Why?' I asked without having a clue as to where this discussion was headed.

'Do you know about the shop that is next to her clinic?'

'Yes, a pharmacy shop,' I replied, totally confused.

'Do you know who that belongs to?'

'That shop belongs to Papa.'

She started laughing at me like I was the biggest idiot. It made me a little uncomfortable.

'No! That land not only belongs to your papa, it belongs to you too.'

It took a few minutes for me to register what she was trying to say. Suddenly a different version of the story and a different version of Soha flashed in my mind.

'So she wants to own the shop and expand her clinic?'

She raised her eyebrows and said, 'Everything I never told you, my son.'

24
Roshan

I was in my room, caught up in the web of my own thoughts and worries when my eyes landed on the black Murphy radio box. A thick dirt layer had been set over it, announcing that it had not been used for a long time. I removed the dirt and tried to tune in the radio. I landed on a channel after changing several stations. The RJ sounded euphoric and I wondered if it was a radio channel or disco studio. The channel played some unheard songs. The vibration and energy in the song made me realize that I was way behind my generation. I flipped through channels again and tuned into Vividh Bharti. RJ Ameen Sayani was on the radio, announcing about the Colgate Cibaca Sangeet mala program. The Geetmala was a weekly countdown show of top filmi songs from Hindi cinema. A smile ran on my face; it seemed Vividh Bharti had banned themselves from changing with time.

A slow sad song of Mukesh was being aired. I was entertained, as there was no one to stop me. I was lying on my bed like a corpse and everything was either emotional or motionless. I started thinking about my father. Why he was so strict? Why did he hate Muslims? Or did he never hate them and it was just Soha's father?

A few years later

It was a busy day, and Papa was deskbound on the front counter, managing the cash. I was helping and guiding the staff in stock keeping. An ambulance came to the Noor Clinic. The ambulance was not a new thing outside a clinic, but the rush was. The crowd kept increasing outside the clinic, and soon, there was a rush. Papa gave the charge of the cash to me and moved towards the clinic. I was looking at the clinic, making my own assumptions.

I wanted to go and see what was happening, but I could not leave the shop. Then I saw a miserable Soha getting down from a car with her mother and almost running inside the clinic. I was married, but still, my heartbeat fastened every time I saw Soha.

My father returned after a while and sat at the cash counter. The downcast face and drooping shoulders were rare on him and he looked at me. The look of regret on his face forced me to ask, 'What happened, Papa?'

'Dr Khan passed away.'

'Oh! But it seems like something else is bothering you too.'

'Dr khan's only son is stuck in Germany. He is in the middle of his exams and cannot come for his last rites.'

'Then who will do it?'

His looked down, without answering.

'Let's close the shop for today and tomorrow,' was all he said.

'Tomorrow also?' I couldn't understand.

'Yes, he was the doctor who never charged any fees from me.'

I never knew he respected Dr Khan so much, or maybe his death had led to a different realization.

I came home and Manisha was busy in the kitchen. Admittedly, I was more worried about Soha than Dr Khan.

I remembered her miserable and hurried walk towards the clinic. I wanted to meet her. However, I knew she was not mine now and I had no rights on her. The next day, the shop was closed and I made an excuse for an evening walk. After changing a few lanes, I was in front of Soha's house. There were three cars and four two-wheelers parked outside.

I thought Soha was alone, but the parking lot indicated that she had more well-wishers than I thought and I was not required.

We opened the shop the next day and I was surprised that Noor Clinic was also open. I enquired from the guard, 'How is the clinic open? And who is the doctor?'

'Dr Soha is here.'

I was amazed by Soha's courage to open the clinic. I thought I would visit her, but somewhere, I failed to do this most basic thing.

It had been five days since Dr Khan's demise. Noor Clinic was running as if nothing had happened. On the sixth day, Soha got down from her scooty and walked towards the clinic, but suddenly turned to face the shop. She looked at me for a second and then looked at my father, gesturing a Namaste. Papa smiled back with genuine greetings, raising both his hands to bless her.

She stepped inside the clinic.

Meanwhile, my father looked at me and flared his nostrils, 'Did you even ask her how she is doing?'

I could not believe that my father had said that. 'We are not on talking terms, Papa.'

'You studied with her, she spent her childhood with you and you are saying this?'

Suddenly the enmity, differences and all trivial things had vanished. I could only see a human being. Respect ran in each pore of my body for my father. I went to meet Soha with my father's permission for the first time.

Soha was sitting on Dr Khan's seat. Her gesture silently said that she was shattered, but had yet not surrendered.

'Can I come in?' I asked still holding the door.

She looked at me and welcomed me with a smile.

'Wow, Roshan.' She guided me to the sofa in one corner of the office.

'How are you, Soha?' I asked settling on the sofa.

'It took six days for you to ask this?'

A lump had formed in my throat. I felt so small.

'Sorry, Soha.'

'Don't worry.' She said changing the topic. 'How are Manisha and Anuj?'

'They are doing well.'

'How is your business doing?'

'As usual, we are struggling with growing competition.'

'Yes, competition is rising.'

I had some thoughts in my mind and I knew I had the authority to say them to her. However, I had been holding it in for a long time.

'Soha, can I advise you something?'

'You want to advise me to marry?'

I laughed. 'Looks like everyone is saying the same thing to you?'

'You are the eleventh person who is suggesting me to get married.'

'Why don't you listen to the eleventh person then?'

She smiled. 'I am not ready for marriage right now.'

'Soon it will be too late for an alliance.'

'You know, in our Muslim community, most of the girls get married even before twenty-two or twenty-three, but my father never forced me to marry.'

'Because you were studying.'

'No, he wanted me to have a respectable life. He wanted to see a doctor in me.'

'You have already finished college and now you are a certified doctor.'

'But I am a daughter as well.'

Was she talking all illogical things, or was I in the wrong frame of mind? There was a knock at her cabin door and a nurse peeped in saying, 'Dr Soha, we need to move for the OT. The patient has gone into labour.'

'You guys arrange everything, I will be there soon,' she replied.

I understood that I should leave. I stood from the seat along with Soha. As I turned to move out of the office, Soha said, 'Roshan, I had three men in my life. One, my brother, who went to Germany, the second one married as per his family's wishes, and the only person who always stood by me, my father, is no more. He had a dream to expand this hospital.'

I liked my new Soha. She was a confident and courageous daughter, not a struggling woman.

'All the best Soha. I am always with you.'

I wanted to hug her, but wondered how she would react. She came near me and hugged me. 'Thanks for coming. We can live without marriage, but we cannot live without a friend.'

I realized yet again, how important I was to her.

25

Anuj

I rushed out of the house to the nearest Metro and boarded the first one that came. The train was flooded with people. Right opposite my seat, there was a man who was clad in a white kurta and a white cap. His outfit screamed that he was a Muslim. I looked at him. He looked completely normal to me. Next to him was a pujari with sandalwood paste on his forehead. It occurred to me that it was their outfits that were making them appear different. On reaching my destination, my eyes landed on Noor Clinic and the pharmacy next to it. I looked at the shop; it was the same shop where Dadaji sat for years. This was the only source of earning for us. I stood there for a few minutes and then dragged myself towards my father's house. Somehow I had never thought that the house belonged to me. As I knocked on the door, I thought why I was there. If the letters were really from my mother. I knocked again and Papa opened the door.

'Oh, Anuj! It's you.' There was no happiness on his face. He did not move and looked like he was worried about my being there so suddenly. He did not even hug me.

'Did I disturb you?' I asked to be sure of what was happening.

'Absolutely not! Why would you think like that? Come inside!'

I went inside and understood everything. Soha was sitting on the sofa. For the second time, it looked like I had entered someone else's house.

'How are you Anuj?' asked Soha.

'I am fine.'

I stood there for a few seconds and Soha understood that she was unwanted.

'I am getting late for the clinic, I must leave.' She picked up her bag and went outside.

No one stopped her. Papa went outside and came in after a few seconds. I made myself comfortable on the sofa.

'How are you?' It was clear that he was not prepared for my arrival. 'Would you like some tea?'

I looked at the cups on the table. I shook my head.

'What happened? Why are you so quiet?'

'Nothing Papa. Do you have something to eat?'

'How about Maggi?' he offered.

I nodded. I was not hungry. I just wanted to check if he had prepared something. I wondered how he was managing everything so easily.

My eyes landed on the documents kept on the table. I looked through the document, but failed to understand anything clearly. It looked like a power of attorney on someone's name and then I read it further. It was a power of attorney under my father's name. I kept the document back on the table.

He came out after about ten minutes and I wondered why they had mentioned two minutes on the pack.

We both sat down to have Maggi.

'How have you been, Papa?'

'Good.'

After eating in silence for a while, I asked him, 'Could you share the next letter?'

'How was the Maggi?' my father asked as if he hadn't heard my question. Somehow I had not even bothered about the Maggi.

'It was delicious.'

He was continuously looking at me, like watching me eating Maggi was the most important thing in his life. Earlier, I had been angry on him. Now, it was replaced with concern.

'Papa, what about Mom's next letter?'

'You are supposed to finish the task before reaching the new one.'

'How can you say that I have not finished the task?'

He watched me with a blank face.

'I have already finished the task, Papa. Why are you doubting me? Didn't I do the previous tasks too?'

'Because you are not answering me.'

'Why should I answer it? It was a task given by my mother. It's between me and my mother.'

He took a long breath and understood that it was hard to reason with me. He went inside and came along with the letter. I took it without any display of emotion and placed it inside my pocket.

'So, is this the last letter written by my mother?'

He nodded.

'Papa, I was thinking we should sell the shop.'

'Why would you say such a thing?'

'Uncle is willing to pay a huge amount for it,' I said.

'Which uncle?'

'Alisha maasi's husband.'

He took a long breath and said, 'Actually, I have a different buyer for the shop.'

'Who?'

'We can talk about that later.'

His discomfort confirmed all my doubts. I understood his helplessness.

'Papa, why are you working so hard to convince me? I know what the next task is and who has written it out for me.' He looked at me with a blank expression. 'Papa, I respect your feelings for her, but you must think about whether she is really interested in you or your shop.' I offered unasked for advice.

'Shut up!' He shouted at me. 'That is none of your business, Anuj.'

This couldn't be happening. My father had not shouted at me even when I had failed in class sixth. He was always a soft-spoken man, but somehow it seemed like he had changed over time and he was not the same man anymore.

'You are thinking too low,' he returned to his normal tone within a minute.

'I can see something which you never would.'

'Really? What can you see?' My father seemed to be getting angry again.

'Leave it, Papa. No more games. I know who has written the letters and the reason behind these tasks. Please stop working so hard to convince me. Stop using my only friend Gagan.'

26
Roshan

I had a rough day at court, where I had shown up to manage some notarized work. I often used to get some commissioned work that needed to be coordinated with the Registrar, even though I was not very regular. I was not keeping well from the last few days as I had been facing some breathing problem. It seemed to be getting worse. I was feeling exhausted and tired again, and was barely able to sit straight without aching all over. Soha had said that she would be coming by the house in the evening, so I decided to take a quick nap before that. But no matter how tired I was, I was unable to sleep. Anuj's fees, Soha's worries and everything else that was happening was keeping me awake. I spent hours staring at the ceiling, thinking about Anuj and our future.

Soha came in the evening with some groceries and medicines. She was a good friend and a free doctor for me. She discussed her worries about the recent big hospitals that had come up around her clinic. It had started to affect her earnings. She also talked about the annoying patients that she had to deal with on an everyday basis. She always got some random requests for illegal abortions, which made her extremely angry. She had never worked for money. All she wanted was a peaceful life, but the way the clinic was struggling under sudden competition, it was worrying her beyond anything about how the business was slipping away from her.

'Are you sure I should expand my clinic at such a time?' she asked me.

I had offered a survival plan for Soha. The dying Noor Clinic could be offered a second chance, if they could expand a little.

'It was originally your idea,' I emphasised.

'Yes, but... do you think we should do it now?'

'Yes, I am sure you can pull it off.'

She thought for a few seconds. Honestly, it was not the first time we were discussing this plan. We knew Anuj had to approve this plan as well since he was the equal owner of the land where the shop was.

'I don't think this is the right time to ask Anuj,' Soha said worried.

'There will never be a right time, Soha,' I said putting the documents on the table.

'But will he agree?'

'This is the only way to stand against the competition, else everything would fall.'

'I do have another option.'

'What is that?'

'If I sell the clinic, I can take that money and join my research program in Germany and join any medical institutes in India afterwards.'

'But you have worked so hard to build this clinic. Why would you give up everything so easily?'

'I think I am a good doctor, but not a good businesswoman.'

'Yes, I know but...' I took a long breath.

'What?'

'I have a weird feeling that if you go to Germany, you will never come back.'

'Why do you say that?'

'Did your brother ever come back from Germany?'

Before she could respond to that, there was a knock at the door. I looked from the peephole and found Anuj on the other side of the door.

'Anuj is here!'

Soha almost panicked and colour drained from her face. We knew that Anuj would not be pleased to see her.

I reluctantly welcomed him inside and when he walked in, he looked at Soha and almost refused to take a seat.

She understood and took leave immediately. I looked at him. He was clearly angry and had a lot of questions. Anuj asked for something to eat, and I offered to get him some Maggi, although there was not much in the house to offer.

He accepted the offer and remained seated in the drawing room. I noticed he was checking the papers on the table. I served the Maggi and looked at my son while he ate. I was so exultant to see him like this, sitting right there, so close to me.

'Could you share the next letter?' he asked coldly.

I doubted he had finished the last task because it was scheduled for Sunday and it was still Wednesday.

There was something weird about his behaviour, but it seemed he was only here for his mom's letter.

I gave the next letter with lots of apprehensions. I somehow understood he was not going to follow my next task. I had a bad feeling about it.

Suddenly he said something unexpected and made me uneasy. 'Papa, I was thinking that we should sell the shop.'

For a moment, it felt like he was aware of what I was planning. I did not like the way he had suggested it. I enquired how he got to know about the shop and other things. He answered vaguely and I could guess it was something spiced up by Alisha. But everything went out of control for me when he indicated that he felt Soha was actually interested in the shop. The harshness and implications of his words nearly made me lose my cool.

I shouted at him, probably for the first time ever. I had never done that in the past. I was never an authoritarian father. He left angry and I knew I had lost our father-son relationship. What went wrong was visible to me. He was ruled and owned by Alisha. I failed to even share what I and Soha were discussing before he showed up. Suddenly it looked like the game which I had initiated was being played by someone else.

I made up my mind. I decided not to give up or surrender. I needed to fix things that had gone wrong.

I picked my mobile and dialled a number. When the caller picked up the phone, I spoke, 'Hi Gagan! You told me that he will visit the church on Sunday!'

27
Anuj

It was Sunday afternoon. I was busy reading a college email on my mobile. Classes would be starting in a few days. I was gearing up for it, and was in the process of making lists of stuff I would need to buy or pack. To start with, there was a huge list of books. I had arranged all my stuff in one place and Papa's fourth letter was lying unattended on the top shelf of the almirah.

I was angry with him for all that he had done. He had played with my emotions, that too for Soha. How could he! I looked at my mother's portrait and saw her smiling face. Then I resumed working on my phone and noticed the battery was getting discharged repeatedly. I got worried a little thinking I will have to shop for a new phone as well.

There was a tall shadow at the door. It was Gagan. He walked in without permission. He came close and stood directly in front of me.

His hand rested on his hips and his stare was sharp. 'Why did you lie to me?'

'What are you talking about?' I asked, confused.

'We had a plan to visit the church on Sunday?' he questioned.

'Yeah, but I went on my own on Tuesday.'

'At least you could have informed me.'

'So that you could inform my father?' I accused.

He did not react, but I read his face. It was a face ashamed over the revelation of his secrets. He sat on the bed and turned his face away from me. I understood that he had done all that with good intentions, to fix the gap between me and Papa. And now, I needed to fix things with him. I couldn't afford to lose him.

'Initially, I wondered how my father got to know that I was coming over to meet him, about how you knew the exact places and exact people that I needed to meet. I also wondered how my father knew that I needed money, that too on the same day when I had asked you to lend me some. I knew clearly that my father could not be so perfect. You must have been helping him.'

There was silence. He failed to make eye contact, which said a lot. 'Why are you so upset with me, Gagan? I should be the one to be upset.'

He did not say anything. I had never seen him so quiet and silent. 'Gagan, when I lost my Mom, frankly speaking, I had only one thing to hold me strong. And it was the fact that I had a best friend with whom I could cry and share my grief. When my father started going around with Soha, I still had a silver lining that I have one person who would never cheat with me. But you also went and joined in the silly stupid game that my father had crafted to play with my emotions.'

He turned his angry face at me and spoke, 'You know what's the best thing about your father, why I decided to help him? Because he loves you. No one is stopping him from getting married, but he wants his family to be with him and I stood by him because that was the right thing to do.'

'You don't know the truth, Gagan. I know why Soha is doing all this...'

'You know nothing,' Gagan said angrily.

'I know she wants to take over our shop, our only source of survival,' I spat in disgust.

'Oh! And who funded the medical expenses when your Mom was struggling?'

'That's not the point...' I started saying, but there was silence in my head. 'Who told you all these things?' I asked him.

His fist was clenched hard and it looked like he was amassing courage to speak. Just as suddenly, I had lost my smiling friend. I wondered what happened to him. I had never seen him so overwhelmed with emotions.

'You know Anuj, my father refused to send me to a good engineering college. I am being forced to join BCA because he could not afford the engineering fee. Your father, who has never been a good earner, is sending you to such an expensive college. You always had the best coaching institutes and best tuitions...'

It was hard to connect the missing dots. But he wasn't the one to lecture me on it. 'So what's the point? I'm on sale? Or my father is...'

'Are you dumb, Anuj?'

'No! But just tell me... does it sound right that a rich lady helps me or my father?'

He shrugged. Everything seemed so obvious to him.

'When did my father tell you about my fees, by the way?'

He smirked at me.

'Could you please answer me?' I asked again.

He replied with the same stupid signature smile of his, 'Always ask the right question from the right person.'

⌘

Soon after, Narendra Modi was announced as the prime ministerial candidate from BJP for the second time. He decided to file his candidature form Varanasi. There was a huge coverage across the media and it seemed that the entire media was chanting about Modi. There were celebrations around Varanasi.

Meanwhile, it was chaos at Alisha maasi's home, with so many people coming to visit uncle, who was a key member and an active politician holding an important position. Uncle was so busy that we barely saw him. If he wasn't busy with his meetings, he would be travelling. The house had turned into an office, and to make it worse, the never-ending renovation was at its peak.

It was dinner time and maasi and I were having dinner together. The best part about her home was that we always ate together. That was the only time when she kept her phone aside, but not before clicking a few pictures and uploading the best ones on her Instagram story. Uncle was missing again from the dining table because of all the election campaigning.

'Can I ask you something, Anuj?' maasi asked as I was about to take my first bite of the dinner.

'Sure maasi.'

'Is there something that is bothering you?'

I frowned. 'Well, there *is* something that is bothering me, auntie,' I said without knowing how much she would understand my concerns.

'Well, why don't you share it with me? I have been asking you for so long. I always say it's better to die in clarity than continue living in confusion.'

'Only on one condition, auntie. You will have to listen to me patiently.' I said this, knowing very well how she would react on hearing about the letters and the tasks I had been doing. She smiled and nodded her head in affirmation. This gave me the courage to ask.

'Who managed all the expenses of my mother's treatment, when she was struggling with cancer? It must have been really expensive, wasn't it?'

'Well, I think you know, Anuj. Take a wild guess! That rich con girl must have funded that.'

'Which rich con girl are you talking about?'

'Soha. Who else?' Maasi's expression had gone sour in a second. It was as if the mere name brought anger to her. Not wanting to aggravate it further, I kept silent and continued digging into my dinner.

Her words made me think, though.

'What happened? Why are you staring at me?' maasi asked.

'Oh nothing, auntie. I was wondering, if Soha was so cunning, why didn't Mom ever say anything against Soha? Why did no one talk ill about her?'

'Your mom was an impractical woman,' maasi said.

I almost dropped my food for a second. I did not like her random comment on my late mother. 'Why do you always talk against Soha? Why do you hate her so much? And now, even for mom?'

She stopped eating her food. She took a long breath. 'Don't you see what is happening? She started coming close to your father when you were about to turn eighteen because she knows that by coming close to you and your father, she can get you to transfer your rights on that land to your father and then eventually to her.'

I looked at her with a blank face.

'Have you ever thought why your grandfather made you and your father the equal owners of the shop?'

'Why?'

'Because he knew that your father had a soft corner towards that con girl.'

Her words made sense. It seemed that my father, mother, Soha and the entire world was conspiring against me. I finished my dinner in silence, but my mind was anything but silent. It was bombarding me with so many questions.

'Was my mother a religious woman?'

'You are asking this question because of your father's letters, aren't you?'

'How did you know about the letters?'

'That is not important.'

'So Gagan told you everything, didn't he?'

She shrugged. I felt cheated by everyone.

'Manisha always had faith in god, but later on, she was hugely frustrated and stopped worshipping altogether.'

'Why?'

'Do you have the courage to hear her exact lines?'

'Yes.'

'She used to say that there are so many gods around us and yet no one was helping her when she was dying in pain. It was pointless to worship.'

Maasi choked on the last words. I ground my teeth, clenched my fists in frustration and left the place.

It seemed I did not know my mother too well. With so much going on in my head, sleep was still far off. Unable to sleep, I walked to my cupboard and grabbed an old album. In one of the pictures, my mother was smiling along with Alisha maasi. She looked so confident and exultant.

Just then, my phone buzzed with a new WhatsApp message, *Goodnight son.*

I looked at that message for at least ten times before replying.

I started typing, *Miss you*, but erased and retyped, *Goodnight Papa.*

I saw his WhatsApp profile picture. It had the three of us – him, mom and me. I looked at the picture and asked myself, 'Is it some other plan his mind is working on?'

My father never puts any status on his profile, but today he had. It read: 'Loneliness is the biggest punishment.'

I rubbed my eyes and took a deep breath. I kept my phone on the table and switched off the lights. Somewhere I was impressed by my father's elaborate plans and efforts on how he had planned so many things, and the intent behind those letters. He had even roped in Gagan. Then I remembered the last letter. I had angrily thrown it inside the cupboard, without even opening it. I woke up quickly and switched on the light. I dug out the letter and started reading.

Hey Son!
This time, you need to go and explore.
Why are there so many gods in Hinduism?
Go to Varanasi and meet Electric baba.

Note: Always ask the right questions from Electric baba.

That rang a bell in my head. Without thinking much, I dropped a message to Gagan.

I am booking two train tickets to Varanasi for us in the Shiv Ganga Express.

28
Anuj

We went first to Dashashwamedh Ghat, Varanasi since it was closest to our accommodation. It was flooded with garbage and tourists. People from all over the country came here to take a dip in the holy river Ganga to wash off their sins. Though now it was not advised as the water was highly polluted, dirty and filthy due to several sewage disposal points, and perhaps all the sins it had washed till now.

These ghats were full of temples. Almost every corner had the picture or statue of Shivalinga and Nandi. I noticed a four-faced Shivalinga there for the first time.

Varanasi lacked basic amenities such as sewers, clean water, and proper electricity distribution, but even then it had come a long way from what I had heard and read in books. The city still had awful roads, but they were being repaired sluggishly with proper drainage solutions and electrical cables were being laid everywhere.

'We have to be very conscious before asking anyone about god. Folks here are too religious,' I cautioned Gagan.

'Yeah, I remember. We need to find the right person,' he repeated the line from the letter.

There was a Banarasi thug tea seller who was captivated looking at us, as he mixed boiling milk and tea masala in a rare passion. He was not even looking at the tea pot. The proficiency and smile said he had been doing the same business since the very inception of Varanasi.

Gagan passed a sly smile and the tea seller smiled back. Gagan walked towards him. It was not shocking to see this behaviour.

'Do you know Electric baba?' Gagan asked.

He smiled and his black teeth gave me a strange feeling. 'Everyone is a baba here on the ghats, sir.'

I looked at him, dissatisfied. He asked me, 'Do you want tea?'

The way he had asked, it looked like he would only share any information if we bought tea from him. 'Two teas please.'

He gave us tea and said, 'Are you looking for Electric baba?'

'Yes,' we both almost jumped up.

'Do you want biscuits as well?' He was clearly a good businessman. We took two biscuits.

'There is an Electric baba at the Blue lassi wala. People usually call him crazy.'

'Why is he called Electric baba?' Meanwhile, we had already finished our teas.

'Do you want one more tea?' I nodded with hesitation.

The tea seller passed a winning smile, like he was dying to answer this question.

'Once a high current electric wire had fallen on him. He was in the hospital for many days, and after the seventh day, he woke up, all recovered. He returned to the ghat and announced that there is no god and people started calling him crazy baba. He was always very arrogant.'

'Is he an intelligent man?'

He looked at me and pointed towards the biscuit jar. I had had enough tea and biscuits for this morning.

'No more tea or biscuits...' Both me and Gagan said in unison.

⌘

When it comes to street food in India, Varanasi has a lot to boast about. Situated on the banks of the river Ganga in Uttar Pradesh, Varanasi is one of the oldest cities in the world, and its street food is as elaborate as the city's history itself. There was an entire street dedicated to a wide variety of street foods.

With little struggle, we reached the Blue lassi wala shop that the tea vendor had mentioned.

The Blue lassi wala apparently was a popular stop for all those who looked for fresh, creamy and flavoured lassis and it had around eighty-three varieties to offer.

I approached the counter and enquired, 'Do you know about Electric baba?'

'Do you want lassi?' he replied without even paying attention to me.

My stomach was still coping from the two cups of tea I had to gulp down to extract the information. I knew it couldn't handle lassi right now. But even before I could say anything, Gagan said, 'One dry fruit lassi please.'

Apparently, he too understood that to get to Electric baba, we needed to make some sacrifices.

The lassi was made with fresh cream and garnished with fruits and chopped pistachios. Before Gagan could finish, I immediately asked, 'Do you know where we can find Electric baba?'

'My uncle *is* Electric baba...'

'Where is he?'

He pointed towards the first floor and said, 'You will find him on the first floor, but do not touch his feet.'

'Oh! Why so?'

'He is a crazy man.'

I had understood by now that everyone in Varanasi was different. But I wondered why his relative would refer to him as crazy so openly. We both took the stairs. Somehow I was too excited to see him. We reached the first floor and there was a warning board outside the door.

'Press the bell only if you are ready to accept that there is no god.'

Gagan and I looked at each other. Gagan shook his head as if warning me that we were about to commit the biggest mistake ever. I summoned all my audacity and rang the bell. An old lady opened the door and signalled us to go inside.

Inside, there was a man who was busy reading a book. He was dressed in boxer shorts and a T-shirt. There were three foreigners next to him, who were also busy reading books.

His room was an opposite picture of Varanasi – organized and peaceful. I had not seen people like him so engrossed in reading. The room contained shelf after shelf filled with books categorized under different genres, almost like a library. There was non-fiction, fiction and even a few books authored in other languages like Russian or French. The room looked like a mini-library.

Electric baba was a clean-shaven man and there was a glowing confidence on his face. I understood he was the man, but still I enquired, 'Sir, can we meet Electric baba?'

No one replied and I asked again, wondering why people wanted to be asked the same thing more than once here. 'Can we meet Electric baba?'

'Am I not looking like a baba to you?' the man said suddenly.

I nodded with a fake smile.

'Please sit!' He directed us to sit on the soft and beautiful carpet. Then he asked us, 'Why have you come here?'

'We have some questions.'

'What kind of questions?'

'Like, why does Hinduism have so many gods?

He smiled. 'Why should I help you? What I will get in return?'

It seemed nothing was free in Varanasi.

'What can we give you?'

'A promise?'

'What kind of promise?'

'You will write a book and talk about me in it.'

'I have no plans of writing a book, but if I ever do, I will write about you.'

He passed a sarcastic smile. 'Now tell me about your question in detail.'

'Why are there so many gods in Hinduism while all other religions have just one god?'

'Folks,' he clapped his hands and caught everyone's attention, 'Gather around!'

All three foreigners joined us on the carpet.

'He is asking an interesting question,' Electric baba said suddenly, quite enthusiastically.

It looked like we were in a gurukul and Electric baba was unfolding life's hidden secrets. Before he could start the rare speech on life, there was a melodic sound in the room. It caught my attention. Electric Baba went to switch off his alarm. He opened his fridge and pulled out a greenish liquid from the fridge and started drinking it.

'What is that?' Gagan asked the pupil who was sitting next to him on the carpet.

'That is bhang,' the pupil replied.

He had the greatest Varanasi invention in his hand. He gulped down the entire bhang in one go and burped out loud.

'Can you ask your question again?' he said after finishing his drink. One of the disciples offered him a white towel and he used it to clean his face.

'Why does Hinduism have so many gods?' I asked while he took a seat.

'Where is god?' he asked me and I went silent. 'Have you ever seen god?'

I shook my head. He pointed to Gagan.

'Have you seen god?' Gagan simply stared back at him with a blank face.

'Sorry to say, our question was different. I wanted to ask, why do Hindus believe that there are so many gods?' I interrupted so that we could get him back to the topic.

He took a long breath. 'Do you think 'Hindu' is a religion?'

'Yes,' I said, thoroughly confused now.

He heaved a deep sigh and prepared himself for a long speech.

The word "Hindu" essentially comes from the word Sindhu. Anyone who is born in the land of Sindhu is a Hindu. It is a cultural and geographical identity.'

That was a completely new thought and Gagan jumped in with his own question.

'So, as per you, I am also a Hindu?'

'Anyone who lives between Hind Mahasagar and Sindhu river can be called a Hindu.'

He confused us further and our silence forced him to speak.

'There is no particular god or ideology that you can call as the Hindu way of life. You can be a Hindu irrespective of whether you worship a god or a goddess, whether you worship a cow or a tree. If you don't worship anything, you can still be a Hindu.'

'If Hindu is not a religion, then why do Hindus worship so many gods?'

'That is known as the theory of illusion.'

'Illusion?'

'Yes, illusion. How can you believe what you have not seen?'

I pouted and rubbed my face, but still, my question remained unanswered.

'I am not asking whether there is a god or not. I am asking why Hindus worship so many gods.'

'Hindus follow a democratic form of religion.'

'Democratic?' That spun my head completely. Not just the government, now religion was also democratic!

Gagan looked at me and we both silently understood and concluded why people called him crazy. I thought it was useless to talk to him anymore. We both started to get up from the carpet in order to leave the place as quickly as possible.

'Wait!' the baba stopped us.

'I still have not answered your question completely. I was just checking your reaction.' We sat back down to hear him out.

'See, all Hindus worship one supreme being, though by different names. There is a reason behind it. People of India hail from different languages and cultural backgrounds, so they have also understood the concept of one god in their own way. For instance, for the followers of Shiva, that one god is Shiva. For the followers of Shakti, or the goddess, the goddess is supreme. Similarly, for Vishnu followers, it is Vishnu.'

This was definitely not something I had expected, but it did make me think.

'Don't you think it's special how our culture gives people the freedom to choose their gods... maybe create a god you can most understand. I think everywhere else, people believe that god created us. We are the only ones who know we are creating our kind of gods each day. So people worship whatever aspect of nature or life they benefit from the most, or relate to the most.'

'But what if we choose a wrong god?' I asked interrupting him.

He smiled. 'Hindus worship the qualities of god. We worship Ram because he was an ideal man. We worship Hanuman because he was the loyalist. We worship Krishna because he was the most intelligent man. We worship the punishing qualities of Durga. We never worship god or miracles. We worship qualities.'

In Varanasi, people upheld religion and god at a very high position and it was shocking to see someone who was religious enough that people called him baba and yet he claimed that there was no god.

'I'm confused...'

'Why are you confused?' he asked.

'If there is no god and humans have created them, then why do so many people believe in god?'

He closed his eyes and it seemed to me like the bhang had started winning over the situation. His disciples were listening with rapt attention.

'You can read all the scriptures and follow the things which are common in all of them.'

He smiled and came near me and touched my head. It felt like he was blessing me. He simply just stood there and smiled with one hand over my head.

'Then we have to read the scriptures? It will take years to understand the truth,' I said in confusion.

He clapped and laughed awkwardly. The clap was a signal. His disciples started to leave the place and Gagan and I sat there confused.

He smiled and nodded.

'What is the conclusion?' I finally asked.

'There is only one absolute truth. Religion is manmade. There can be hundreds of religions but...' He took a pause as he was having hiccups which were interrupting his speech

'There is only one god.... Or no god.'

29
Anuj

Dashashwamedh Ghat is one of the main ghats in Varanasi on the Ganga River. It is located close to Vishwanath Temple and is probably one of the most visited ghats. It was the aarti time and our last night in Varanasi. There were thousands of people attending the Ganga aarti. The Ghat was full of pilgrims. A group of young pundits wearing saffron robes conducted the aartis. Sounds of conch shells echoed in the air and incense sticks gave the whole place a serene yet pleasant fragrance. All the ghats were lit with numerous lights and enhanced further by the lights from the lamps.

We were sitting at the corner and watching the aarti ceremony. The unclean Ganga flowed with pride in the background. Finally, I had understood what my father was trying to say all this while.

I looked at Gagan. He was trying hard to keep himself calm. I understood that Electric baba must have shaken his beliefs as well.

'Why are you so fidgety?' I asked.

'This is so hard to believe.'

'Yes. But I guess what he said was the truth too. But what exactly is bothering you so much?'

'How could someone call him crazy?'

I fumed.

'Are you seriously thinking about that?'

He nodded. Here, someone had shook my entire faith and he was bothered with just the word crazy.

'We are leaving tomorrow. Have you finished the entire task?' Gagan asked.

'Yes, I now understand what my father has been trying to say.'

'Really? What is that?' Gagan asked surprised.

'There is only one god and my father wants to make me understand, that in reality, it's useless to think about the differences. All religion, arts, sciences are mere branches of the same tree.'

'What does that mean?'

It was hard for him to digest all this. He thought for a few seconds and almost shouted. 'Means *all* those letters were fake?' Gagan asked, 'I thought at least one letter would be by your mother.'

'Of course they were all fake. That is the whole reason why my father used you.'

'Your father used me?' He swallowed hard and his fallen shoulders and disgusting face said that he could cry anytime. I looked at him and thought, 'He used you for the right thing, but for the wrong reason.'

I did not say it out loud, because I doubted that he would understand it.

'So where is the original letter?' Gagan asked.

'My mom never wrote a letter for me.'

'But how is that possible? Your maasi, uncle, mamaji and even your Canada-based cousins got a letter from her. How could your mom miss writing a letter to you?'

I gave it deep thought and his words made sense. I had found a new mystery to solve. I rose from my seat mumbling, 'Why she did not write to me? There are things that she never told me.'

30

Roshan

'What? Are you serious?' asked Soha surprised. 'He went to Varanasi even after knowing everything?'

'Yes,' I replied. Somewhere I was contented that my son had gone to Varanasi. But I wondered whether he would reach Electric baba or not. He was the only person who could clarify his doubts. I had been to this place way back, while on a trip.

'How did he react when he got to know about your counterfeit letters?'

'I have ruined his trust, Soha.'

'I already warned you about not doing something like this.'

'I know. It was not a good idea. He knows that all those letters were written by me and I had planned all of this, but he still went to Varanasi. I guess, somewhere, I have still not failed as a father.'

'So what do you think is going inside Anuj's mind?'

'I don't know'

'What next?'

'I think the time has come for us to make a decision.'

I know she was an egoistic lady. Her decision was final in many cases. Before she could announce any verdict, I asked, 'What have you thought about the hospital?'

'I am already in touch with brokers. I guess selling the hospital is the best option. It will be easy for me. Staying here seems difficult.'

'But why? I am sure Anuj would agree. You can expand your hospital.'

She made a sorry face. 'I'm not only perturbed about whether he would agree or not. The losses are high and selling is the best option.' Then she paused and collected her thoughts. 'Can I ask you something, Roshan?'

'Why are you asking my permission? Is it something that bad?'

'If you need to choose between me and your son, who would you choose?'

'What kind of a question is that?'

'Just answer the question.'

I did not take much time. The most loved face was in front of me. I said, 'I cannot afford to lose either of you.'

31
Anuj

Alisha maasi's house had taken on more grandeur and luxury than ever before after the renovation. I had begun to think that the renovations would never end, but it did and the house literally sparkled.

Her Instagram was flooded with posts about her new house that showed everything from wall paintings to decor items and even taking questions related to which colour would go well with the sofa and which colour would suit the walls. Maasi had taken the renovation project to a different level through her social media platforms. She was running a giveaway contest on Instagram where winners would be receiving a prize on answering which colour best suited her newly-renovated temple. The prize was an idol of Goddess Lakshmi. Surprisingly, when I checked the mini temple, it was already coloured in saffron. The contest was just to create a hype.

Two days later, she started another contest. This time it was to answer which lord should be placed on the top shelf. She made an extra space to put a big Shiva statue and other gods and goddess were moved to the lower shelves. I looked at all other gods and felt sympathy for their sudden change in positions.

It seemed that even after the renovations, work was still in progress as I found both auntie and uncle in a heavy discussion on the colour of the curtains. They were discussing whether they should change it in order to match the new temple. I decided to go back to my room. Just as I was leaving, Alisha auntie called me.

'Hey Anuj, I need a few minutes from you. Come here.'

I was sure that she was calling me for my opinion on the colours of the curtains or the position of the coffee table. I didn't want to face her wrath, so I gently dragged myself to her.

'We are thinking of colouring the entire temple in reddish yellow.' She was carrying a colour booklet and pointed at a series of coloured boxes, 'What do you think? Which shade would look the best?'

I thought I was seeing double, or suddenly I had gone colour blind, because all I could see was boxes and boxes of yellow colour on the page and all of them looked just the same. I didn't know how to pick a colour when everything looked the same.

'But it's already coloured saffron?'

'That is just for election purposes. We will click some images and have some interview shots in front of the temple and after that, we shall change the colour.'

I looked at the temple and suddenly I had sympathy for all the gods, including Shiva.

I looked at the booklet again and spent a few seconds looking at the yellow boxes over and over again, till I suspected myself of having contracted jaundice just by looking at these yellow boxes. Having had enough, I handed the booklet back to maasi.

'Choose the one you feel is the best.'

'I liked this one, but your uncle is saying this one.' She pointed to two of the boxes.

I understood what I needed to do. 'Go for this, your choice is perfect, maasi.'

She passed a winning smile. Sometimes we fool ourselves by asking a question. We know what we want. I was about to walk away, but she called out again.

'What happened to you, Anuj? You have been gloomy ever since you returned from Varanasi.'

'Nothing like it. Have just been thinking about something.'

'Care to share with me?'

'Why do you need a temple when god is everywhere?'

'How can you question god, Anuj?' she looked shocked.

'I am not questioning god, auntie. I'm questioning the need for a temple. There's a difference.'

She came near me and touched my head. Her motherly touch told me that she had no answer for my question and this was her way of avoiding an answer. I felt bad about having put her in a tough position with my question.

'What happened Anuj?'

'Nothing maasi, just wondering about my mom.' I changed the topic to a more relevant one.

'Oh, my son!' She hugged me. 'So you are missing your mom?'

'No, I am not missing Mom. I'm wondering how it is possible that my mom has written a letter to everyone, but not to me.'

'That is no surprise. She has not written any letters to your father as well.'

'But why?'

'I guess, she believed that those whom she loved the most, didn't need such formalities or gestures to prove her love.'

'Can I see the letter that my mom wrote to you?'

She looked at me, displeased.

'That is personal, Anuj.'

⌘

Papa, Hope you are good. I'm coming home today evening. I texted papa on WhatsApp.

It was not that I needed permission to go to my own house, but I did not want to face Soha. I dressed in a red T-shirt and blue jeans and walked towards the metro station. I boarded the metro for Rohini. As I took a seat, I looked outside at my city and started comparing everything with Varanasi. That's when I realised that I was still living in an illusion.

I got down after half an hour. My eyes landed on our shop and Soha's clinic. There was something unusual happening at the clinic. Someone was removing the board of Noor Clinic. I assumed that perhaps like maasi, the renovation bug had gotten into Soha too, and the clinic was getting renovated. But still, something seemed odd and I decided to check it out. I went to the man who was removing the board and enquired, 'Why are you removing the board?'

'This hospital has shut down. So we are getting rid of all the old stuff.' There was a newly painted board that was lying on the ground.

AVAILABLE FOR SALE

There was also a number mentioned below for queries. It was my father's number. I was not surprised. Soha perhaps didn't want to share her number publicly.

'Why is she selling the property?' I asked the man, who had by now ripped out the entire board.

'I have no clue. I think the hospital was not doing well.'

I reached home and my father extended a warm welcome. The drawing room, sofa and dining table, everything was clean.

We exchanged greetings and shared some updates about Alisha maasi and how her home renovation was going on. He smiled and said, 'Don't worry! She would be renovating her house again next year.'

I passed a sarcastic smile. I was waiting for him to initiate a chat related to my Varanasi trip. But he did not ask anything.

'Would you like to have some snacks?'

'No, I have brought something with me,' I said, offering him the samosas that I had picked up from his favourite shop. Without waiting for anything else, we both dug into our samosas, giving it our full attention. I took a look at my father and I could see that there was a smile on his face. He was definitely enjoying his samosa. Thinking it to be the best time, I asked, 'Papa, why is Soha selling her clinic?'

'That clinic is not doing well. Recently a big hospital opened up in the area. It is offering a sea of facilities under one roof and people prefer that to the small clinic.'

'Oh, but didn't she have plans for expansion?'

'Yes, she had. But later on, she dropped that idea. It is majorly because of funding issues. She does not have enough funds.'

There was a lump in my throat. 'Now what will she do?'

'She is going to Germany next month for some research for two years, and when she comes back, she would join a hospital. I'm helping her sell the land.'

Meanwhile, we had finished the samosas. He took our empty plates to the kitchen and started washing them. I went to the kitchen to help him.

'Don't worry, I got this. But can you get the clothes? I had washed them in the morning and they have been in the washing machine. Can you please help me put them out?'

'But it's evening now, Papa. Why did you leave it until now?'

'Actually, I have some pain in my knee and it was a little difficult for me to climb the stairs.'

'Why don't you hire a full-time maid, Papa?'

He did not reply and I went to the washroom, picked up the clothes and went to the roof. All flats in our area have a common roof. All the people who stayed in the building shared the same roof. When I went there, one of our neighbours, Aparna auntie was also there. I offered the usual pleasantries to her.

'Hey Anuj, when did you come?'

The question was an indirect taunt, I could sense, implying that I had moved out of my home.

'I had just gone for a vacation to Varanasi.'

'Oh, got it!' She said with a smirk on her face. 'So, are you doing well?' There was a strange enthusiasm in her voice.

'I was always good.'

She faked a smile. 'Do not hesitate to call me, if you need anything.'

I started drying the clothes to stop her from going on and on.

'I don't need anything, but in my absence, if anyone can help my father, it will be great.'

'Why? What happened to him?' she smirked. 'Doesn't he have the best doctors to take care of him?'

I glared at her. I quickly finished drying the clothes and rushed back into the house. I had an awkward empathy for my father. How was he tolerating so much from everyone, including me?

'Papa, I want to talk to you,' I said as soon as I saw him coming out of the kitchen.

It seemed my father had aged a lot while I was gone. He looked weak and much older now. He came to me and kept his hands on my shoulders. I touched his hand back because I knew he needed me more than ever before.

'I always doubted that those tasks and letters were written by you, and after finishing them, I realized I'm not the same person. I never thought I would say this, but please go ahead and marry her. Or just leave her completely, but please choose a respectful life.'

There was a smile on his face.

'But I have one condition. I will not meet you at this house, whenever she is here.' His expressions changed suddenly. 'This house will belong to you both.'

'Why?'

'I have spent my entire life seeing you with Mom.'

I could see my words had hurt him, and I felt bad for being so blunt.

'But Papa, you do the right thing, even if it makes you feel bad. The purpose of life is not to be happy, but to be worthy of getting happiness.'

He raised his eyebrow and took a step towards me. I stepped back a little, saying graciously, 'Papa, I don't want any discussion on this topic anymore.'

He gazed down and there was silence for a few seconds. I understood that this was the best time to share the things that I was carrying in my mind.

'Papa, where are Mom's original letters?'

'What are you talking about?'

'How is it possible that Mom has written a letter to every relative, but not to me?'

'No clue, son. I had asked the same question as well. Many times.'

'What did she say then?'

'She did not say anything,' he hung his head with those words.

I stood there, checking his facial expressions to see whether he was lying. Because it sounded so unlike Mom. But his eyes said that he was saying the truth. It was pointless to discuss anything. So I went to my room and started packing my things. I had to be in the hostel room next week, to take charge of my accommodation before college started. My father came to the room.

'When is your college starting?'

'Monday.' I asked again without turning to look at him, 'Can I carry some utensils from here?'

'You don't need my permission. It's your house, son.'

I picked a few things from the almirah and some from the kitchen and realized that the size of my bag was getting bigger and bigger. When I was almost about to leave, I thought of asking, 'Papa, suppose at any moment, if you need to choose between me and her, who will you pick?'

32

Roshan

When I received the WhatsApp message from Anuj that morning that he would be coming home, I was not surprised. Last time when Anuj came home, he had met Soha. I could see it was not a comfortable situation for Anuj. It was clear on his face that he had hated it.

I was excited about meeting him. I had started taking a few notary works again recently. I spent a few hours writing some legal notices and client declarations. The knee pain was not allowing me to walk much. Since I did not have a habit of watching TV, I spent my time looking at my walls, while my mind swallowed itself with all kinds of troubles and worries.

Anuj came in the evening with samosas from my favourite shop. His sweet gesture was enough for me to keep my worries at bay. It seemed that the Varanasi trip had worked. I could see a new glow of confidence and freshness on his face.

We discussed many things related to Alisha and her house renovation and laughed about it too. It had been a long time since we had talked and laughed together like that. I wish I could hold time. I wanted to ask him about the trip, but somehow I hesitated to initiate the discussion. Gagan had already informed me about what had happened during their meeting with Electric baba.

When I asked for his help to dry the clothes, he came back really angry. I did not know what went wrong there. He came up to me like he had made a decision and said emotionally, 'Please go ahead and marry her. Or just leave her completely, but please choose a respectful life.'

Yes, those were the words that I had always wanted to hear. But he said those with a gloomy face and a small voice. I wanted to say so much, but he stopped me. I could see that he had made up his mind. It was heartbreaking when he said he had seen me with Manisha all his life. And he could only see Soha as my partner, and nothing else. He cannot see me with another woman, and that, I guess, was the most genuine answer he could give.

He asked about his mom's letter. The same question had bothered me too, for so long. I had always wondered why Manisha never wrote anything to him. Or did she?

Anuj got busy packing his stuff for college. I did not like the fact that Anuj had felt the need to ask for my permission to pick something from the kitchen.

I had my son with me after such a long time. We hugged as he got all set to leave for college. One look at his bag and I knew he did not want to return home.

There was sadness on his face and the guilt of hurting me. It looked like he was planning to leave forever. But right then, before leaving, he asked me something.

'Papa, if you need to choose between me and her, who will you choose?'

I looked at him intently, and saw myself in him. He had started resembling me gradually. The sadness on his face also reminded me of many things from my past. Neither he nor I had been like this. We also deserved to live with smiles and happiness, like other families. So much had changed between us. I loved him more than anything else in the world, but it seemed I had failed to express my emotions.

'Anuj, when I was growing up, I lost my love and my confidence. And when I had grown, I lost my wife. Losing your wife is not just losing a person; it's like losing an entire family. Don't even think of comparing yourself with anyone, son. You are that part of my life which I am the most proud and possessive about. If ever I need to choose between you or anyone else, I will have a clear choice. It will always be you. Only you, my son.'

He hugged me for a few seconds and when we let go of each other, I noticed he had tears in his eyes and a long lost smile.

33
Anuj

I left from my house and headed towards Gagan's place. He lived in a predominantly Punjabi colony in Govindpuri. I had crossed ten lanes and five blind turns to end up in his neighbourhood. There were many small lanes in the colony and these lanes were so narrow that only people could come in – cars were a distant dream. After fifteen minutes of walking and running around the maze-like lanes, I finally reached Gagan's house. There was no privacy in his house. It looked like the entire locality was peeping into each other's houses. Everybody was curious about who came and went into the neighbour's house. Aunties were staring from the roof and windows of their homes. There was someone always fighting in the neighbourhood. Sometimes it was for parking, sometimes it was garbage and other times nobody knew the reason – including the people who were fighting.

I reached his house and knocked on the door. His father opened the door and even before I could offer greetings, he shouted, 'Gagan, your friend Anuj is here.'

Gagan came with his hair open and flowing around. I was amazed to see his long hair as I had always seen him with a turban. For a moment, he looked like a lady with a moustache and beard. It was clear that my sudden presence at his home had made him uncomfortable and worried at the same time. There was a big question mark on his face. He invited me inside.

'Are you free?' I asked.

'He is always free.' His father shouted from behind.

'Give me a minute. I will just get ready.'

I now understood why he never invited me to his house. I sat on the edge of the sofa. His father sat just opposite me and kept staring at me. I diverted my gaze. It had been quite a while since I had been to his house. There were too many things in the drawing room – TV, a rack full of show-pieces, a box-shaped bed, another rack full of trophies, and another one for photographs. It was a wonder that they had left the floor alone, because every inch of the room was jam-packed with things.

There was a big family picture with six sardars, all dressed in a white turban. Just as I was staring at the photograph, Gagan's father's voice boomed, bringing my attention back to him.

'You want tea or coffee?'

'No uncle. I'm fine.'

He was cautiously observing me and there were clearly some queries on his face. I was wondering when Gagan would come so that I could escape his father's scrutiny.

'What were you guys doing for three days in Varanasi?'

'We just went for a small holiday before I join the engineering college next week.'

'So you are going for engineering?'

It was hard even to nod as I realised what I had done.

'I wish Gagan could also do something like that. I don't know why he is wasting his time with friends. Roaming all the time. Sometimes in Varanasi, sometimes at some mosque.' He sighed with exasperation, 'Chasing some useless Punjabi girls.'

I gulped uncomfortably.

He picked the remote in anger and unmuted the television. My attention was also diverted to the TV automatically. The movie *Hum Aapke Hain Kaun*, starring Madhuri Dixit and Salman Khan was playing.

'He is wasting time watching such useless movies,' uncle said in disgust. I realized Gagan must have been watching the movie before I came.

Gagan's father had just started his encyclopaedia on the many ways in which he was disappointed with Gagan, when Gagan came running down the stairs and saved me from further torture.

'Let's go.'

Gagan and I ran as fast as we could from his home. For the first time, I felt sorry for him.

'Why are you so silent?' Gagan read my face.

'Why does your father always scold you?'

'That's every father's job. Just ignore.'

I had never seen my father like this. My father never complained about anything, and just like that, it occurred to me that I had been so lucky to not be with the worst.

'What happened? What are you thinking about?' Gagan asked as soon as we took a seat in a cafe close to his neighbourhood.

'Oh nothing, just coming from home.'

'Oh, you went to meet uncle?'

'Yes.'

'Did he give the real letter written by your mom?'

'No, it seems there is no letter. Papa is not aware of any such letter.'

'Did you check with your maasi?'

'I don't think she has it, because if she did, she would have shared it with me by now. I mean, what's there to hide?'

He nodded and ordered two teas for both of us.

'Why does Alisha maasi hate Soha so much?' Gagan asked like a detective.

'I don't know. I always wondered why she behaved like that. It feels like she even hates my mom sometimes.'

He kept sipping his tea in silence, pondering over the whole puzzle. I was sure he was my true friend, because he hadn't given anything in life so much thought. He finally finished the tea and I went to the counter to pay the bill.

'Is there a possibility that your maasi had a crush on your father?' Gagan asked abruptly.

I looked at him, shocked. 'Could you please stop watching Hindi movies? It is getting to your head.'

'How do you know I was watching a Hindi movie?'

⌘

I reached maasi's place. This time she was busy choosing which smart TV would match the carpet, and at the same time, look good on the wall. I guessed it was a small worry, considering that she had a long list of more such concerns.

The biggest worry in her life right now seemed to be the dark-coloured sofa which was already on its way, but posed a threat as to whether it would match the TV and the carpet.

'Hi Anuj! Where have you been?' she asked while uploading a picture on Instagram.

'I went to meet Papa.'

'Oh. All well?'

'Yes, nothing special. I just went to collect a few things.'

'Okay.' She handed over her phone to me and asked, 'Can you please click a picture, like I am reading this book?'

I nodded and took the mobile from her hand. 'Shall I focus on the picture, on the book, or at you?' I said adjusting the mobile phone to the perfect angle.

'Of course on me. The book can be blurred.'

I took a few pictures with some candid poses of her.

'*You Are the Best Wife*, along with coffee. How is that for a caption?'

I nodded and wondered, what was so special about the book. 'Have you read this book – *You Are the Best Wife*?'

'No... just sharing an image with the book. Reading books seems to be in vogue right now, and it's a beautiful cover too.'

Fools are spreading their intelligence around the world and intelligent people do not care about anything. I clicked some more pictures of her and she quickly got busy uploading them on Instagram. I knew she would blast me for this, but I still couldn't stop myself from doing it.

'Maasi, I want to tell you something.'

'Yeah? What?' she continued looking at the phone screen.

'I know about the letter.'

'Which letter?' her head shot up suddenly.

'The letter which you have been hiding from me all these years.' I took a blind shot.

She flushed. Almost immediately, she lost her cool and composure. 'Who told you about it? Your father?'

Oh my god! Was she really hiding something? I played along. 'It doesn't matter. Where is the letter?'

'This is nonsense!' her voice was loud and shrill, perhaps for the first time ever.

coreyhouse
267   44.98
www.coreyhouse.com

'Let it be, but I really don't care.'

'Let me tell you, your mom has not written any such letter,' she said and almost stood up.

'How can you say with such confidence?'

'N... No... I am... You are unnecessarily...'

She started stammering and sat back on the sofa. Her eyes were compressed, tense and focused. She pursed her lips and licked them twice. It appeared that her throat had gone dry. Her breathing was shallow and she rubbed her open palms against her thighs, perhaps to wipe off the sweat.

I went close to her and held her shivering hand in mine. I asked softly, 'Where is my mom's last letter?'

There was silence for a few seconds. I understood she knew very well about the letters. She started looking at her phone and I could see that she was trying to avoid the topic.

'Why do you hate Soha aunty so much?'

She stared at me and her eyes broadened with a stern look. She took me by surprise when she yelled loudly, 'Don't you dare talk to me like that ever again.'

But I wasn't going to let it go. I asked the question again, a little more forcefully this time. 'Where is the original letter, auntie?'

She took a bottle of water from the table and gulped large sips of water, taking an awful lot of time too. It looked like she was preparing herself for the unpleasant discussion that was sure to pop up.

'You know, your mother was an impractical lady,' she said.

I did not react except for perhaps a question mark on my face, which clearly said I would not settle for anything other than the letter. She moved towards the almirah in her room and pulled out one big bag, searching for something. My whole body was struggling to stay still. I could have pounced on the bag and looked inside myself. She took out two envelopes and opened one of them, but instead of giving me that, she gave me the second letter.

'What is in that letter?' I asked pointing at the one she had kept with herself.

'That is my sister's letter for me, and the one you are holding is the one that your mother wrote for you.' Her voice was laced with anger.

The envelope I had in my hand was a bit thick. I opened the envelope with a lot of anticipation. I felt a sudden warmth engulf me, as if my mother herself was seated next to me. I felt her presence. I scanned the letter. The writing was hard to read. It looked like some kid had written it.

'Who has written this letter?'

'Manisha,' she said a single word.

'It's not my mom's handwriting. I know her handwriting.'

This was the only letter she had written with her own hands when she was struggling in the hospital. The rest were written by your father, but dictated by your mother. She had written this letter when she was really sick.'

I looked at the letter and tried to imagine the pain that she must have gone through and how she must have struggled to write this letter for me on the hospital bed. How her hand would have shivered in putting down all these precious emotions. How she must have decided to write on her own.

I folded the letter and without saying anything, ran to my room. I locked the room. Mom's photograph was hanging on the wall of my room, and she was smiling, as if nothing had happened.

I read the letter.

Dear Son,

I am sure I would be long gone when you read this, but I really wanted to tell you what you mean to me. You are the only portion of me which will live even after I am gone, and you must know that you meant everything to me.

Ever since I was a child, there were a lot of struggles in my life. But, you know what, everything was nice, because I always had a loving family with me.

When you came into my life, it changed in so many ways. It gave me a reason to live... to make a difference.

I had grown up in a society of differences. I was always taught that there were Hindus and then there were Muslims and that we both were different. I decided my son would never be known as a Hindu or a Muslim. That is the reason I didn't want you to have a surname, so that people would never judge you based on your name.

I am sure you are mature enough to understand about Soha. She was not just a doctor for us, her dues could never be compensated. I always had a respectable life, but with growing medical expenses, I could not ignore the support and kindness that she had shown to our family. I know no one would ever agree with me, but I hope my son would. It's the hardest thing for a wife to say, but son, you need to help your father rebuild his life after I am gone. You have to make him understand that he is not here to live for others, but for himself too.

My stay in the hospital has made me realize that people are more helpful than god. If you love, you will be loved; if you will respect others, you will get respect. We need to show more belief in people rather than someone superficial who we have never seen but we blindly follow.

Your father and I have raised you with a lot of love, and also hopes. I always wanted to see a better version of your father in you. Stop believing in miracles, because if it has to happen, it will happen anyway. Just don't forget to give it your best shot.

Anuj, I will never be able to put into words how pained I am to know that I won't see you grow. But always remember, I will be watching over you. You are the only one I have loved so selflessly, and so has your father. What he has done for us, not every man would have.

Son, always remember, whatever life we live, in the end, we are all just memories.

Make beautiful memories.

Love,
Mom

I read the letter again and again. I realized my legs were shivering and my throat had gone dry. I had tears in my eyes. I picked the frame that held the smiling photograph of my mother and hugged it firmly and mumbled, 'Please hug me once, Mom. Please hug me once.'

34

Roshan

S oha came to the house to see me. It was uneasy for me to accept that she was leaving and we would perhaps never meet again. As a last gesture of kindness, I asked her to make me a cup of coffee. Unlike her usual self, she was quiet and didn't nag about the unclean utensils or the condition of the kitchen.

Once the coffee was ready, she poured us two cups.

'My education loan got approved,' she said.

'That is good news,' I said taking a sip of the delicious coffee I was going to miss.

'Yeah, but they need a guarantor who could fund, in case I turn out to be a defaulter. I have to submit lots of documents, and guarantor details too.'

'Can I be the guarantor?' I offered.

She smiled. 'No, my brother will manage that.' She had the coffee in silence.

'Will you rent my flat in my absence?' she asked.

'Yes, but what about the furniture that you have?'

'I am thinking of keeping all the furniture in one room and locking it. The rest of the place could be easily rented out to a small family, I am sure.' She had thought this through.

'Yeah, it seems like a good idea.'

'You had brought something for me to eat, na? What was that?' I asked, remembering that Soha had brought with her a large tiffin box.

'Oh yes! Just a minute,' Soha jumped up and went into the kitchen. She brought back the tiffin box, opened it and I couldn't help myself from smiling.

It was sheer khurma.

'Wow!' I took a large scoop. 'It's delicious. Nothing has changed even after so many years.' I said with a huge smile. It was heart-breaking to know that she had said hello to me with sheer khurma back in school one day, and she was here to say goodbye with it too. I wondered why god had made my life so dramatic.

As I ate, it dawned on me that after all those years, once again, I was losing my best friend and the best partner. It was déjà vu watching her for the last time as we said our goodbyes.

'Finally, the time has come... again,' she said.

I nodded as I asked, 'So, are we meeting for the last time?'

'Surely not the last time, we...' she failed to complete the sentence.

'Once again you are going for higher education, and you will become a very big doctor.'

She smiled.

'Did you get any buyer for the hospital?' I tried to change the topic.

'No, everyone is paying half the market price because the hospital construction is so old.'

'It's a perfect place for a restaurant. Shouldn't you try that?'

'No, I'm thinking of selling it to some bank.'

I nodded in response. There was no point in delaying the obvious.

Soha got up from the sofa and started moving towards the door. It seemed my entire life was flashing past in front of my eyes. We had known each other for so long. I never thought she was a stranger or someone different from me. Soha smiled as she opened the door to leave. No one can understand the guts it takes to lose everything and still have a smile on your face.

'Wait, I also wanted to gift you something,' I said suddenly.

I pulled a book from the table and gave it to her. She looked at the book and read the title loud, '*You Are the Best Friend*, a true love story.'

'Since when did you start reading books?' Soha asked mockingly.

'Lots of free time now, so I thought I should start a new hobby.'

Her expression changed suddenly as she said, 'I have a request to make. Please do not discuss anything with Anuj.'

'What is there to discuss?'

'About me selling the hospital and you planning to sell your shop for me.'

I simply nodded.

'Would you call me from Germany?' I said, agonised to bits.

She was standing still and started looking at the floor, trying hard not to cry. I thought of asking something, but knew it would make her weak. So I restrained and ate up my words.

'Take care, Soha. Sorry I failed to convince my son.'

She looked at me and there were tears in her eyes. 'No, Roshan. It's wonderful when someone tries even after knowing the result.'

I couldn't see her crying. She had always been the strong girl, so I went close to her and we hugged. I did not say anything and she did not say anything. I lost track of how long we sobbed like that.

35
Anuj

I woke up in the morning with my mother's photo still clutched to my heart. I placed it back on the wall and checked my phone. It had three missed calls, one from Papa and two from Gagan.

I called back Gagan first.

'Hi Gagan! Is your father at home?'

'Yes, why?' he questioned, confusion and sleep dripping from his voice.

'I need a small help from him.'

'No, please don't come to my house.'

'I will be there in an hour,' I said and hung up.

I had a glass of juice, picked some documents related to my birth certificates, address proof and my Aadhaar card and walked out of the house.

I took the Metro and reached Gagan's house. His father appeared to be on his way out in his advocate's attire.

'Namaste, uncle ji.'

'Hi, Anuj.' He welcomed me and went inside to collect some of the belongings.

'Come to my room.' Gagan invited me into his room and almost dragged me with him, but I forced myself out of his hold.

'I need a small help from your father.'

Gagan gulped his saliva. He whispered, 'Do not involve my father into this. I have already had enough because of you.'

Meanwhile, his father came. 'Yes Anuj, how are you?'

'Actually, I came to meet you.'

He frowned, so I quickly told him, 'I need a small favour.'

He nodded. 'Tell me.'

'I wanted to understand what a power of attorney is?'

'Why?'

'Actually...'

Before I could say something, he started speaking. 'I'm in a hurry, so let me explain it quickly. A power of attorney or POA, as we call it, is a legal document giving one person the power to act on behalf of another person. It is used in the event of someone's illness or disability, or when the person can't be present to sign necessary legal documents for financial transactions.'

'In that case, can you make a power of attorney for me, uncle?'

'I can... but whom do you wish to authorize in your absence.'

'My father.'

'And for which property?'

'Me and my father hold joint ownership of a property and I wish to give the entire signing authority to him.'

He sighed and looked at Gagan, 'At least you have something to give to your father.'

I didn't know what to say, so I waited for him to speak again. Finally, he said, 'Okay, but I need a lot of documents.'

My father was an advocate, and I knew.

I said in confidence. 'I have all the documents with me.'

⌘

Gagan came with the power of attorney that was now in my father's name. I was collecting some of the documents when Alisha maasi came to my room.

'So you are doing it?' There was a taunt and worry on her face. But I could also see the maasi who had concern for me. I went near her and hugged her.

'Auntie, my mother was lucky to have a sister like you.'

She was struggling to breathe and when we went apart, she had tears. She exhaled and controlled her emotions and said, 'You are a good son, Anuj.'

I smiled and saying my goodbye to her, left the place for my home.

On my way home, I looked at the greenery and construction around Delhi. Everything looked so amazing. It felt like a burden had been taken off my head. Delhi metro was flooded with people. With every station I crossed, I was flooded with memories. I remembered how my father used to accompany me during my exams. He was always there to support me.

I reached Rohini sector 16 metro station. I got down and my eyes landed on the pharmacy store, and then I looked at the Noor Clinic. This had been struggling for years. I took a rickshaw towards my house.

A known lady got down from an auto-rickshaw and started moving towards Noor Clinic. Suddenly something struck in me.

I almost shouted to the rickshaw puller, 'Please stop!'

'Sorry bhaiya, I have to get down.' I paid him ten rupees, but he made an gloomy face. I gave him ten rupees more and he was satisfied.

There was a big sale board now instead of the clinic's name. I went inside and as soon as the attendant saw me, he queried, 'Are you looking for a doctor?'

I looked at him. He seemed to be new as I had never seen him before.

'Are you a patient?' he asked again.

'Yes, I want to consult the doctor.'

'She is in the middle of her namaaz. You will have to wait for a few minutes.'

I nodded and sat on the iron chair. The clinic had never been so silent. It appeared that there was no one except Soha auntie and this man in the clinic. The water dispenser was removed and there used to be a big sofa in the lobby, which too was missing. There was no furniture now, except for a few plastic chairs.

Soha auntie got free a few minutes later. The attendant went inside to inform her about me and when he returned, he said I could go inside.

I took a long breath and asked, 'Can I use the washroom first?'

He nodded and I let him guide me to the washroom, even though I knew where it was. I knew almost every nook and corner of the clinic. I went to the restroom and looked at myself in the mirror. What was I going to say to her? I had just walked into the clinic on an impulse and wasn't actually looking forward to meet Soha auntie.

I came out from the washroom and reached her cabin. I knocked at the semi-transparent door. 'Please come in,' Soha auntie's words echoed from inside the almost empty cabin.

I opened the door. 'Oh Anuj, it's you! Please come, I thought it was some patient.'

'Namaste auntie.' I did not say Soha ji. A lot had changed in my heart.

'Please sit. Is everything okay?' she enquired with worry on her face.

'Yes.'

I looked around her cabin. There were many awards and decorations on the walls. It was the only portion in the clinic which had not changed in years. I could see her attachment to the clinic in these small things.

'Are you alright, Anuj?'

'I have been suffering from something for quite a while now.'

'Oh! Feel free to share.' She was hearing me with rapt attention.

'I heard that you are planning to sell the clinic?'

'Yes, I'm actually going for higher studies. But don't you worry about all that. It's been taken care of.'

She was still trying to hide her problems.

'Actually, I came here for my mother, auntie.' I found it was a little tough to speak.

'Go on, Anuj. You can share anything with me,' she said lovingly.

'My mother always wanted you to expand the clinic. She took her last breath in this hospital and...' there was a lump in my throat '...I would be obliged if you can take the adjacent land from my father and...'

Before she could say anything, I put the papers I had got from Gagan's father on the table and said, 'Here is the permission.'

She looked at the power of attorney, her face almost devoid of any expression.

'But why? I mean, why would you think that your mom wanted me to expand the clinic?'

'I don't know. I guess, she was an impractical lady.'

'No she was not...'

'It doesn't matter anymore, auntie. I would be obliged if you could fulfil my mom's wish. Could you please take the full ownership of the adjacent plot from Papa? I made him the signing authority for the property.'

'That is between you and your father, Anuj. You kindly give this to him yourself.'

I nodded and got up to leave. I had something in my mind and that must have been visible on my face as Soha auntie called me back.

'What are you carrying in your heart, Anuj?'

'Why did you do so much for us?' I said, almost in a reflex.

She frowned.

'I always thought my father was a rich man as he never let me feel that we were a poor family. When I grew up, I thought you owned this hospital and were surrounded by servants. I assumed you were a rich lady and didn't need anything in life. Whenever I met you, you always got candies and chocolates for me. I even asked how my father managed everything when my mother was struggling with a deadly disease. I realize now that you helped my father in every stage of his life. It was only a few days back that I got to know that the clinic is not doing well. That things have changed.'

I heaved a sigh.

'Why have you done so much for my family and why do you love my father so much?'

She was silent and took her time to speak. 'I never thought I was doing a favour to anyone. I did it because I thought it was my duty to take care of my best friend's family.'

The word 'family' echoed in my mind. It'd been ages since I had known what a family is.

'I have a request to make,' Soha ji said.

'Yes please...'

'I am leaving India and it would be great if you could move back with your father.'

I nodded.

'Your father loves you, Anuj. I'm so sorry for creating all the mess around your family. You are a good son, Anuj.'

I looked at her tearful eyes, and in that moment, I did not see a Muslim woman or a doctor. I saw a mother.

She left her chair and came close to me.

'I have a request to make,' I said chocking on my own words.

'Please tell me.'

'Please do not leave the country... we need you.'

'No Anuj. You need your father, not me.'

'No, I need a family, not just my father.'

There was a question mark on her face.

'I need a mother too...' I summoned my courage and said, 'It's been years since I got a hug from my mother. Can I hug my...'

Soha auntie wrapped me in a hug even before I could finish my sentence.

'Oh, my son!'

I closed my eyes and we hugged each other. I continued, 'I missed you, Mom. I missed you for so many years.'

Epilogue

A few months later
Soha dropped her plan for future studies. Noor Clinic got ready to expand to double its size. Now it was a leading hospital in Rohini.

Their wedding was arranged in an Arya Samaj mandir. We invited Alisha maasi and uncle too, but we knew they won't be coming.

It was a very small and secular wedding. There was a Sikh friend, and a Muslim bride, with a Hindu groom. So it was obvious that none of the usual rituals of marriage would be possible. So it was a small and simple ceremony focussed on my father and mother.

Seeing my father in the groom's attire was an overwhelming feeling. At the same time, it was also amusing to see worry and concern on his face, just like any other groom. I was a little uneasy to see my father sitting with a woman, other than my mother, but I knew Papa's happiness meant the most. I stood there in front of him to assure him that I was with him.

When the wedding ritual was about to finish, I went to the washroom and opened my mother's letter. I wept, letting go of everything that was troubling me till now. Suddenly the phone vibrated and alerted me to a WhatsApp message.

All Hindus are in danger. Please read carefully:

Why are all Bollywood Muslim celebrities married to Hindus? The list of these celebrities is long, including Shah Rukh khan, Amir Khan, Saif Ali Khan and many more....

I read the first few lines and deleted the message, blocking the sender immediately.

I came out of the washroom and greeted my father, who was now a married man, again.

On the studies front, I opted for Electronic Engineering and finished my first year from BIMTECH. I bought a new phone too. I also made an Instagram account for myself. I was delighted to see Alisha maasi's page active with the pictures of her beautiful mansion. Her latest article was almost trending.

I followed her on Instagram and she immediately messaged me, asking when I would come to see her newly-renovated house. I replied, promising that I would visit her as soon as my vacation started, which I did.

After finishing my first year, I went to meet maasi. She had kept some pooja on account of my arrival. I helped her to organize and decorate the temple. However, I refused to participate in the pooja. She had invited her entire trope of socialite friends. I came out of my room after the pooja was over and the ladies had left the place.

I joined hands and offered my obeisance to god. As soon as I finished, maasi asked with a taunting smile, 'So, who did you pray to? Allah or bhagwan?'

I smiled at her comment and replied, 'Maasi, both are the same.'